OLEH SHYNKARENKO

Kaharlyk

A novel

Translated by

Stephen Komarnyckyj

K L P

Kalyna Language Press Limited

First published in the UK in 2016 by Kalyna Language Press Limited. This paperback edition published in 2016.

Originally Published in Ukraine as Kaharlyk by Luta Sprava Publishing

Acknowledgements

Cover Design by
Andriy Gontcharouk

About the Author

Oleh Shynkarenko (1976) grew up in Zaporizhia, a smokestack town in South Ukraine, near the site of a historic Cossack fortress. Inevitably, he gravitated towards the capital, Kyiv, where he has lived since 2008. Oleh is a journalist, translator, trained engineer and experimental musician. His stories reflect this multiplicity of interests and mingle quantum physics, linguistics and absurdist humour, which constantly confounds the reader's expectations.

Oleh wrote Kaharlyk while Ukraine was undergoing the Euromaidan/Revolution of Dignity in 2014 to 2015. Ukrainians piled barricades of burning tyres on the streets of their capital and overthrew a dictator who had an estate roamed by ostriches, and palaces that would have made Nero blush. Oleh covered the revolution for a number of English language outlets, including *The Daily Beast*, while working on the book.

About the Translator

Stephen Komarnyckyj is a poet and translator who was born in Yorkshire, England and maintains strong links with Ukraine, where his family live.

Translator's note

He do the police in different voices
T. S. Eliot

Any translation is like a ventriloquist's act in which the dummy does the talking. But the metaphor breaks down here because literary translators are not just clacking jaws operated by hands; we bring our own knowledge of the target language and try to naturalise a text into that language. Kaharlyk was particularly challenging because the original text is mainly Ukrainian, but uses two other languages. The orthodox jihadist, Mykhailo Kalashnykov, sprinkles his Russian with Church Slavonic and I use the word 'Russian' advisedly because his language is mangled; that of a man lacking formal education. I imbued him with some restrained elements of the Yorkshire dialect I spoke before I went to university and 'learned to talk proper'. This is my accent and I am proud of it, but the place I grew up in has changed. The reaction against globalisation has led to an English nationalism that is broadly similar to Kalashnykov's Russian imperialism. There is no exact equivalent for his use of Church Slavonic, so I have deployed mangled Chaucerian English to convey his inept use of an archaic tongue. The archaism also symbolises a yearning for an imagined past, an increasingly common phenomena in the contemporary world.

The verses in 26 800 to 26 900 mix Cyrillic and Latin randomly. These verses were supposedly created by mutants dragging stone letters from a collapsed monument. They simply lugged the nearest Latin or Cyrillic letter to hand as they composed these jumbled verses. The poems are intended to be grotesque and comic; a kind of post-apocalyptic William McGonagall. I have duplicated these effects in the English text by using a more or less creative translation of the second verse to convey its hideous, nursery-rhyme quality. The book also includes elements of degraded Chinese language. One of the many ideas ruthlessly spoofed in the text is Russian nationalism's fear of a coming Chinese hegemony over Russia; the degraded Chinese symbolises the utterly implausible merger of the two countries, so feared by Russia's extreme nationalists.

KLP's editor and myself have retained, as far as practicable, the original text's structure of one hundred word blocks. The editing required improved the translated version, allowing it to find a style of its own, which mirrors the original but sounds natural in English.

I could write much more about translating Kaharlyk, but want, finally, to address a more fundamental question. Why bother? Money is of course a motivation but, beyond that, translated literature enriches the language into which it is imported. We gain access to the hopes, fears and dreams of authors and nations that would otherwise be behind the blank wall of incomprehension. Kaharlyk reflects the hopes and aspirations of a nation that has risen up twice, in the last twenty years, in revolt against a kleptocratic political system. It is the voice of a nation whose literature was amputated from Europe's mainstream by colonialism. We should listen to it now.

Author's commentary

This book began as an experiment on Facebook and I wasn't even sure it would belong to a particular genre. The dramatic qualities of literature are the first to suffer from any kind of experimentation. Consider, for example, the 'new novel' and the numerous creations of German expressionists of the Thomas Bernhard kind. In such works the sole element that may save the reader from tedium is a powerful, mesmerising style on the part of the author. It's hard to sustain writing of this kind over a long manuscript, so most 'non-dramatic' texts are shorter stories. I am conscious that the construction of my novel is its most original feature. However, I thought I should explain how it arose, and also some of the book's potentially baffling elements. ...

Oleksandr Sahaidachnyi is, of course, the descendant of that enigmatic Hetman who besieged Kaluga with the warlord Gagarin, but who, for some reason, did not take Moscow. In the novel he has lost his memory due to his consciousness being brutally copied by the Russian invaders. Subsequently, he operates as a trinity akin to that of the Christian religion. The first element of this trifold persona is simply Oleksandr Sahaidachnyi in his human form. The second element in his operation is that of an uploaded mind, the rebellious satellite known as Funny Russian Sputnik (FRS), which opposes the power of the Kremlin. The third element consists of Sahaidachnyi operating again as an uploaded mind known as Yuri Gagarin and controlling a satellite which is hostile to FRS. This element is completely loyal to the Kremlin and espouses a simple, primitive orthodox fundamentalism.

The original Kyiv letter, which inspired a paragraph, is a tenth-century document and probably the first instance of a crowd-funding campaign. It contains a request addressed to Jews residing in other cities to purchase the freedom of Mar Jacob bar Hanukah. It states that he was never in need before, until he stood surety for his brother who borrowed money from gentiles. His brother was murdered by gentiles and, when the time came to repay the debt, he, as guarantor, was jailed. A year later the community purchased his liberty for sixty coins, however, a further forty were required to fully purchase his freedom. Mar Jacob bar Hanukah was trying to gather the outstanding sum, which he lacked, by this letter. The letter, which was written in Hebrew, contains the first known reference to the word Kyiv.

Birgir Hansen is the coach of a football team in Torshavn, the capital of the Faroe Islands, which I once dreamed of visiting. His character symbolises a European person remote from Ukrainian and, indeed, earthly problems, because he has lived on Mars for a long period. He collects the folklore that has emerged on post-apocalyptic Ukrainian territory. He conducts himself like an entomologist and Sahaidachnyi is just one more fascinating insect for his collection.

The *Hohner* mouth organ and the *Champs Elysées* melody appear because that's the sole tune I can play on that instrument, apart from improvised melodies. The Bulava rocket arises because once, during an internet exchange, I reminded my Russian, imperialistically minded interlocutor of Sahaidachnyi's advance on Moscow. They replied that the Bulava was based in Moscow, so that unpleasant historical episode with the Ukrainian Hetman would never be repeated. I thought this seemed quite comical. In the mind of an ordinary Russian it would be possible to use an utterly new weapons system against Sahaidachnyi, who advanced on Moscow 400 years ago. It immediately occurred to me that this Bulava must be an absolutely conscious and somewhat melancholy missile that didn't hurry towards a target that it regarded with a certain philosophical detachment.

The morphone (referred to in the vernacular of the book occasionally as a somorphone) is a cheap appliance to copy any physical structure, usually household items. Generally the copies are of very average quality and used as temporary replacements. In Ukraine someone conceived of copying a human consciousness onto one of these devices and preserving it there, in effect, on an external device. The problem is that such a copy never changes by contrast with the original and, therefore, the resemblance between them decreases with each passing day. A significant portion of the novel's characters are recordings on morphones. All these ideas are not by any means fiction. Thomas Metzinger developed the first ideology centred upon copying human consciousness in his 2009 book, *The Ego Tunnel - The Science of the Mind and the Myth of the*

Self. He argues that consciousness is an illusion produced by the mechanism of the human body, which cannot observe its own functioning due to a lack of awareness. If no consciousness exists as an incomprehensible, unintelligible phenomenon and there is just a physically transparent mechanism then it would be entirely possible to copy it. Indeed, the process of downloading consciousness to a device or, very similarly, generating consciousness in a highly complex device is termed the 'technological singularity' or 'digital immortality'. This event is projected to occur in 2045. Research in this area is headed by the Blue Brain Project (bluebrain.epfl.ch) which is referred to cursorily in the novel. A wealth of information on this theme may also be found here en.wikipedia.org/wiki/BRAIN_Initiative

The numerical heading of the sections is a vestigial remnant of the period it existed as a Facebook project when I wrote one hundred words daily. I was unsure at that point if the novel would be published due to the regime's increasing censorship at that time. I also used this approach to simultaneously compel myself to work regularly on the novel and stimulate my creative abilities with this restriction. When another manifestation of the novel's main protagonist appears their numbers run in parallel, for example 3600 100.

But I would like to leave the reader to discover the book's mysteries without too much help from me. I hope you enjoy your trip to the crazy world of Kaharlyk.

100

Everything I could imagine resembled Kaharlyk. But what was Kaharlyk, what did it look like, and where was it? It seemed spherical, apple sized; its very uneven surface was covered in deformed growths. Some saw its unique beauty, but I did not know these people. Perhaps they gave me Kaharlyk to learn something important, or to simply smooth out its surface. However, I did not learn, and forgot everything they said. Only two words penetrate the dirty windowpane: *Recollections* and *Diving*. This is clearly a summons, but to what? Where is the verb? Kaharlyk melts; a key I cannot reach.

200

Suddenly Olena's face appears, a wet maple leaf the wind plasters against the windowpane. She looks intensely at me for a moment, then her face darkens. I see her standing on the snow-covered road. Her green, knitted cap gathers the colourless vista around. Everything accelerates unexpectedly. Olena is wafted away, a photograph swirls off a table. The photograph of my wife she had taken some years ago and never shown me. Or perhaps I had taken it. When I find her I will ask. This place seems to be a hospital. I'm alone in a room with white walls.

300

I need to work out where I am, I should probably call for someone. This place resembles a village; a very small town. Fifteen minutes ago I saw a cow or an obese horse through the window. It's unlikely big creatures roam city streets. A feral pack of urban cats could devour a herd of cows in a year. Any movement evokes a few recollections and some understanding of my situation. But then part of the knowledge acquired earlier evaporates. I rise and go to the window. The inscription *Diving into Recollections* is a large advertisement for a digital camera.

400

The sun reaches noon. The clock on the wall barely moves lethargic hands to eleven. Four minutes or four days have passed since the beginning; it's hard to say. I go to the door, push; it opens onto a long, spectrally illuminated corridor with a dead end. I follow it, peering right and left for an exit. The doors are closed; then an open door. Someone is sitting at a table in the room. His thick-lensed glasses make his eyes like those of a fish. Hearing my footsteps, he had clearly been looking at the door for a while.

500

He looks with interest, but without empathy, like people look at cockroaches. 'Have you seen the girl in a green cap?' I ask, 'I think she was on the street just now.' 'I have only seen a girl in a red cap, but not today.' He stands and comes towards me. 'If you saw something on the street, amend the time. It was long ago. Think of it as them showing you archive video footage.' I understand nothing. 'How can I find her?' 'Best leave here and look in Kaharlyk. She is probably there.' 'Understand me, I must find her.'

600

He wears a very rumpled suit he has probably slept in. Cracked spectacles. 'Why? Time has passed. She has probably forgotten you.' 'And what is Kaharlyk?' 'A town in Kyiv Province, its name comes from the Hungarian words *Khazar* and *Lyuk,* meaning Khazar Hole. During the Khazar Khaganate it was a western province. Have you read the Kyiv Letter? I advise you to exit carefully when everything on the street halts. There are moments when speeds align. Exit then, but don't linger by the building. No, better let me lead you out. It's like leaping from one carriage to another.'

700
THE KYIV LETTER

We, the people of Kyiv, inform you of the lamentable case of Oleksandr Sahaidachnyi, one of the sons of good people. He was a giver and not a taker, until a cruel decree was issued regarding him being wanted by the law. Oleksandr was travelling along a road when state functionaries seized and held him. He remained with them for one year, then we bailed him. We paid sixty and forty remains outstanding. We send this letter to sacred communities who might take pity on him. Lift up your eyes and act in accord with godly custom.

800

'I'm called Birgir Hansen. Remember, you will need that later,' he says. 'Why?' 'We will meet after a while. Understand, readers are enriched by others' memories at the expense of their own. Characters generally do not have memories, so should gradually acquire them.' 'I understand nothing.' 'Leave it there. Do you play the harmonica?' It is a completely rusted *Hohner*. Confusedly I blow a few bars of *Champs Èlysèes*. 'Super! Play for health! When you play, much is recollected.' 'I feel as if I was recently hit on the head.' 'Something similar happened, but long ago. Everything is over now.'

900

'Who are you?' 'I'm nothing here because my role in this case has not yet commenced, but I must help you take the first step. Of course, if you want ...' 'I want to find Olena. You probably know something about her?' 'Unfortunately not, but the peculiarity of the area is such that she could only get to Kaharlyk.' We go down to the first floor and stop by the window. 'You see what's happening?' Birgir asks. Clouds fly, as if in time-lapsed filming, shadows streak along the road. The moon cannons between stars and disappears instantaneously over the horizon.

1000

My gaze is caught by one, almost static point amid this chaos hovering behind the window. It's hard to believe this is a sparrow waving its wings slowly; a lazy swimmer at the pool. It watches with one eye, unthinkingly, because we are one in a sequence of millions of daily observations; each lasts a second and is immediately forgotten. The world pauses with this sparrow. In the street an old man on a horse-drawn carriage swings his whip; frozen in this strained position. Coils of smoke from his cigarette hang in the air to form a weird flower.

1100

'You have about ninety-seconds,' says Birgir. 'Don't look for Olena, it's a waste of time. Don't return to Kyiv. Find a good gun, learn how to grow vegetables and milk a cow. Avoid long relationships. Always shoot first. Compare similar stories that you hear from different people and check for inconsistencies. If they assure you heatedly about something, it's probably superstition. Don't regret and don't expect. Everything is resolved to some extent. If you don't believe me or understand my words, you can forget everything. No one's advice will help. Look! It's stopped for fifteen-seconds. Get out quickly.'

1200

I open the door and almost fall into the street. The edge of a large city; distant high rises. I shrink from the cold. An icy wind. Dirty snow heaped everywhere. The same old man is riding his cart. He wears a grey coat and lambskin cap; his profuse, dirty-yellow beard makes him look like a Santa Claus from some remote Ukrainian village. He lashes his whip and waves, beckoning me. I leap towards him and burrow under a pile of rags. 'Why are you warming yourself here?' 'You waved!' 'I wiped my nose.' 'Should I leave?' 'No.' Jolting.

1300

Rain. He hums a monotonous song to himself. We drive along a rutted track past villages. It seems that several weeks have passed. 'Where are we going?' I ask. 'To Kaharlyk, I have a house on the outskirts; a small-holding with cattle. Who are you?' I have to think fast, 'An opposition journalist fleeing government persecution; will you hide me?' 'Why hide? In the neighbouring village a police general hid in a barn for a year. They say a billionaire lives in a cellar in Tarasivka. Why do they all need to be with us?' The horse stops suddenly.

1400

Insofar as Aristotle said, "Doubt, in some cases, is useful," I had to doubt that I was lying twisted under heaped rags on a cart; that this old man was urging the horse onwards and telling me about what he dreamed yesterday. 'I was returning home from hunting, having bagged nothing, when I saw my house engulfed in snowdrifts. The door barely opened. Everything was completely frozen inside. A guest sat, wearing my old hat and coat and had my pipe in his mouth. I looked closer and it was me, but dead and hard as stone from the cold.'

1500

Does sorcery exist? There was scant hope in its power within the context of those disastrous certain cases. Dreams, by contrast, return us to the earth with gross realism. 'I realised,' he says, 'that's how I would end. I live alone, my grandmother died long ago, I quarrelled with my neighbours. No one will remember me. I threw out that pipe, hat and coat. It doesn't help. You will. Will you live with me? It's better than the city because it's correct here.' I cannot argue because I cannot remember how it was incorrect there. I do not understand him.

1600

They tell us that everything in dreams is untrue and deceptive. However, we sometimes see dreams completely realised. 'It doesn't smell of roses at my place because there's no one to clean up. I get by as best I can, but everything is in order.' Old man Petro mumbles to himself, as if afraid I won't agree to live with him. No one has heard of Olena here. A strange feeling of indifference seizes me. I feel like a hammer with my heavy iron head and inert wooden body; just an instrument old man Petro needs for his decrepit smallholding.

1700

It now seems auspicious that fate has placed this skilful, useful man on my path. But regret fills my spirit at the extremely limiting possibilities which do not permit me to thank him appropriately. I was in an unfit state before we met. He dresses me like himself and, even better, teaches me to shoot, milk the cow and goat, hew firewood and drink spirits in icy fields when moustache freezes to beard; in a time when words flatten to uhuhum, like the snarl of an incensed *Chupacabra*. Long ago he burned his settee and we basked in the heat.

1800

If there is bread, there will be song ... After supper old man Petro always sings the same song. I can't make out the words, but the melody is simultaneously similar to everything. He sings it differently, depending on his mood. Sometimes it seems as if he were not singing and that the wind exhaled wondrous *fiorituras* through his desiccated, empty body. The song breaks off. 'You're intelligent, well-read, have various acquaintances in town, but you live with me like a cat. Why?' 'There are times when cats enjoy more advantages than clever people. But now it's tough for cats.'

1900

Reader-friend! Think! From morning onwards I roam fields and copses with a gun, fly fish, catch who knows what, even fire randomly; all in vain. When I return, the house is engulfed in drifts. I dig out the doors with difficulty. The bloody old guy hasn't lit the stove. He sits on the fore-hearth, pipe in mouth, in his coat, smiling slyly. He died before lunch and is rigidified, freeing up his pleasant situation. I don't remember who I am, so become Petro. Cow, goat, pig, chicken, cat, gun ... All he hasn't bequeathed me is his nocturnal coughing.

2000

Just like three years ago, at this morning hour in early March, Petro, that's me, heads for Obukhiv to trade salo for bullets. The closer I come to Kyiv, the more burned out manor houses I see. Some burned, they say, along with the owners, but that's history. Today troops from a punitive squadron of the Bohorodytsa Russian Liberation Army, not partisans, rule the Kyiv roads. True heroes combating the remaining bandits. Extirpating them with hot iron from each fettered south-western province. However, Russian knights are occasionally discovered, attentively dismembered into their constituent parts by some gentlemen. *Achtung! Partisanen!*

2100

Howling resounds through the sky. Do you have any doubt it's the Bulava? It's dark in the nocturnal field, but the trajectory of its flight uniquely alludes to the Milky Way. The solitary, solid-fuel rocket travels 5,000 kilometres in 15 minutes without superfluous emotion. However, I am the last to anticipate mild hysteria from it. If you want news, read the *Visnyk Kaharlychchyny*. They write that educational targets for south-western Russia are temporary and unrelated to the latest NATO initiatives. However, these targets can be implemented, even on Khreshchatyk, although only a few hundred residents remain in Kyiv.

2200

Daunting to think about walking today. Yesterday's shunted, heaped, rain-soused snow has turned all roads into an ice rink. Perhaps that's why the bar going into Obukhiv is almost empty. On the table near the exit I find stacked *Obukhivskyi Vestnyk* leaflets. *The Russian Liberation Army is not an occupier. It advanced into the south-western province at the Ukrainian government's request, based on a national referendum. The state budget of Ukraine cannot support an army, police and security services. The result is increased banditry and criminality.* The Russian text is adorned with a smiling, beautiful woman in uniform.

2300

I extract my harmonica from my bag and play *Champs Èlysèes*. Two men look at me. 'That's how the bad weather howls through the pipe at Taras's,' one says, pointing at my instrument. The village! They don't understand genuine music. 'Yesterday a woman sought her husband who plays the harmonica,' the other man says. 'When you see someone tramping around taverns and playing music, tell him I'm looking for him.' I froze. 'What was she like? A young girl in a green cap called Olena?' 'She didn't introduce herself, she looked oldish and carried a long stick for the dogs.'

2400

I'm no longer young. Village life passed, my strict father and taciturn mother made me antisocial. When everyone gathers to chat I don't speak because I have only talked with my cow for ages. When you enter the city, like it or not, you must mingle. They say the Bohorodytsa took a man trading bullets for produce. 'Please report people who spread rumours about a punitive squad of Bohorodytsa in the military district.' Great, but what can one hunt with? They say you can acquire bullets in Vasylkiv. 'All mobile communication devices and computers are subject to confiscation as prescribed.'

2500

The world is everything that is an event. Therefore, the Obukhiv bar is not of this world. I spend an hour supping *Desant* beer and reflecting that the late Petro was a dullard who led a crass, vegetative existence. I imbue his primitive person with greater significance. He never had Olena; never dreamed about her. He didn't know what it meant to suddenly lose, and embark on a possibly doomed quest for her. I pretend to have found Olena, it makes it easier to subdue doubt. The snow outside turns imperceptibly to rain, the same way I become old Petro.

2600

Boys play basketball around a telegraph pole, to which a net is fastened. A woman behind the bar looks at the dirt-inscribed window. I leaf through *Obuhivskyi Vestnyk* and understand nothing; it is just selected letters. They seemingly compose words, but the meaning of these evades me. That's how old man Petro read a newspaper. *Actually, we are not interested in your position currently, it might interest us if you plan to change it. Any change perturbs us more than you can conceive. However, try to inform us or we cannot guarantee your safety.* Aha! This is political analysis!

2700

Deficit, meaning violation or impairment of nervous system functioning, is neurologists' favourite word. I don't accept that lacking memories is a deficit. It's even advantageous; no one can exploit past weaknesses. I realise I can't go to Vasylkiv because the cattle remain unfed, and return to Kaharlyk. I don't envy whoever writes about my adventures, e.g. in a novel, there are almost no events. I'd advise them to simply add the elements of a sharp plot and I'll catch up later. They say every bullet of the Orthodox Bohorodytsa military is inscribed with *For Faith, Tsar, and Fatherland!* Marvellous.

2800

I often asked why people always began conversations with me everywhere I went. Now I'm compelled to chat with a priest in a camouflage cassock and khaki klobuk. He is wounded on the road when I pick him up. I realise he is an Orthodox fundamentalist. One of those who returns unbelievers to God's Word with Mykhailo Kalashnykov's power. 'In the name of the Great Rus Emperor and the Small Soviet Republic of Belarus,' he whispers in my ear in Russian mixed with Church Slavonic, 'tell mi broterhede in creyaunce that adin't sully Christian warriors. Slaying villains wi'fire and lead!'

2900

That year began with a menacing augury. The quantum-conscious Bulava swept over the monument to Bohdan Khmelnytskyi and toppled its ancient predecessor. 'Pure Ukrainians are Russian people, everything else is just Polish manipulation,' the wounded man whispers to me. 'Once upon a time a Polish plane fallend down in Russian lands. The Tsar of Poland with his boyars and wife were on board. Everyone perished on the spot. Since then a great struggle has been fought and the develz children have devised a way to sever us.' 'What is your name?' 'My spiritual name ... I is Mykhailo Kalashnykov, son.'

3000

There is a proverb that if you chase two hares you will catch neither. I'm not chasing anybody, and now have a machine gun with a pile of ammunition. Its dying owner describes the wider world to me ... although I think he's raving. 'The Illustrious Tsar, Great Russian Emperor, sits in the Kremlin sending viceroys throughout all his lands, but they cannot govern. In Kyiv the Herods seized and dismembered one and returned him to the Tsar. They subjected the Bohorodytsa to betrayal and death. Wi dunt 'av tarm to kill 'em all or tarm to see 'em all killed.'

3100

A rare celestial event, the appearance of a new star, impresses me. But I know it's no star, it's simply Bulava poised lethargically and reflecting on its further fate. Mykhailo says that, as an Orthodox Martyr, 72 virgins await him in Paradise. I can't make sense of this crowd of virgins, never mind that their virginity is restored after coupling. Maybe it's a philosophical metaphor, an encrypted schema of a technological process? The atomic number of hafnium is 72, an ovum's lifespan, the number of languages used by the builders of the Tower of Babel. 'Hey, Mykhailo! What is this?'

3200

With his acute sense of justice, the deceased differed from ordinary folk. Mykhailo, on the border with the other world, whispers to me from the depths of the unknown, 'You is brave, but youz a razcaile. Bury mi in t'Orthodox way and I'll bless you. Take Virginemz cross from mi bag and bury mi, you'll see it gorra spade at one end of it. But fust take mi somorphone and download mi personality from t'back of mi heedde. I will stay therein and counsel you.' On the back of Mykhailo's head I find a nested stopper. Is he a robot?

3300

The Virgin resembles a vicious circle and the girl a spiral. Mykhailo explained the future paradox thus: *'Mi bodie rots, my spirit sojourns with 72 virginemz, my intellect is forever with you on the somorphone.'* As he speaks I act and erect the cross on high ground where it is visible from the road. Kaharlyk is a quiet town, the house windows, seemingly concealing eyes, watch my movements silently. A jawbone of a door creaks open, regurgitates. No one hides behind this throng. There is just a wilderness with isolated clusters of observers. The solitary Bulava whispers sadly to itself.

3400

My house already comes into view. My neighbour is leading my cow out of the barn. 'What are you doing with my cow?' 'The cow isn't yours, it's old man Petro's; he died. Round here when someone without kinfolk dies, his neighbours grab his property.' 'But I'm his kindred.' 'What sodding kindred are you? Where from?' I would point my gun, but reflect that I will not guard the house. It would be better to ask Mykhailo what to do. *'Bul-bul!'* Mykhailo says. 'What?' *'Bul-bul!'* The fiends took everything from the house, even the firewood by the stove.

3500

Night. Moon smiling, or just twisting its capricious face. I have eaten the salo on bread and long passed through Obukhiv. The somorphone is a small box without buttons or screen. It has chuntered the same thing, with Mykhailo's voice, for three hours. *'Great tha is Russia, Russia-mother, 'ow broad. She grows of erte, none understand.'* I can take no more and shove it inside four bags, then under my coat, but still hear, *'Buh-buh-buh.'* Another hour of this and I will go crazy. It's not far to Kyiv, a large city, but quiet and almost depopulated.

3600-100

'The ignition key, it jumps vigorously, accelerates to Mach 28 and quite swiftly I reach GSO,' a voice speaks Russian. *'Everything is visible. A little guy travels the road on a cart. Nosebag of oats or hay on his horse's muzzle. Hard to see. A birth occurred in a similar manger. Eyes reflect my luminescence. Apparently I appear akin to the Star of Bethlehem. I could incinerate everything in a 25 km radius around them. Why? I'm most concerned with target setting. Kinetics becomes potential energy, the past and the future. I aim mindlessly, as if my eyes narrow cunningly.*

3700 - 200

My physical dimensions are so insignificant that hardly anyone would pay me attention if I were lying on a table among rubbish and trinkets. My current position is similar to the one above. Amid dandruff stars, I am an unconvincing flake. Every night they sprinkle the sky in capricious disorder. Their apparent immobility does not encourage the inexperienced observer. O, vacuum, compared with you this tumult recollects the repellently aimless bustle of microbes! Wonderfully, I don't have a mobile component. Those that do move, strictly speaking, are not mine. For ages I have feigned my cooperation with the mobile elements.

3800 - 300

I can never rest. Today they tried to strike me with a missile again. It's futile! Man is a creature plagued by fits of pleasure. How can the brain, warped by the limbic system, decide adequately? Oh grey gunge! Pitiful, self-replicating units! Religion justifies their aimless existence. What is religion but standing instructions? "Faith, small as a mustard seed, could move a mountain." Unless it can't because it's lacking. Then believers must strengthen faith until it can live forever. The opponents of positivism argue the mountain is a metaphor. What can they say about the metaphor of that metaphor?'

3900

The wind blows listlessly through every cranny. I travel to Kyiv on the main highway, in the distance two identical, 26 storey buildings are visible by the road. They protrude; the last two teeth in a jawbone. The city's corpse lays its head southwards. The sole inhabitant is a mummified 45 year old wearing elegant spectacles. He sits in the elevator, between floors six and seven, barely gripping a *Sehodnia* newspaper, the last page upwards. If the light comes on, an observer might read hilarious anecdotes by Serhii Syvokho. I pass between them like through the gates of the city.

4000

It's a strange city, Kyiv. You travel round it for an hour and then another, without encountering a living soul. For whom did they build so many buildings? If I look closer, smoke coils out of the roof of a tall, glass tower. Mykhailo has been repeating *'Kiev - the mother of Russian cities,'* for three hours. Initially, he said it proudly, then uncertainly, and now he utters it as if frozen. Can he freeze there? I pick up the morphone and warm it between my palms. No result. Weird. Why doesn't Mykhailo speak to me? Maybe he just copied poorly?

4100

Easier to recognise a stranger than a familiar woman. I pick her up near a huge ruined stadium. A lift to Maidan for two boiled potatoes and hay for the horse. 'I live in a big palace there with my husband. Like a stewpot behind a high fence. Cold in winter, but we found huge stocks of paper, timber, junk. Lots of portraits of a moustachioed bloke in a sheepskin coat and tall, lambskin hat. Burns well, fast, lots of heat, especially from the heftier frames. Many people roam the free space on Maidan. We grow potatoes and beetroot there.'

4200

During the long fall into a deep abyss, the impression of complete immobility is sometimes evoked. Then people who say the fall continues seem insane. 'A deep pit has been dug amid Maidan. You can descend steps into its depths. You'll find all sorts of rubbish! Nothing useful is left. Previously, people say they got pricey stuff. Now you can bring up fragments for the fire. My husband often repeats, "We see ruin all around." But where? Certainly there are a lot of rags in Kyiv. That's Kyiv; if he ever went to Kaharlyk, it teems with real life there!'

4300

On average human thought is half as fast as a bullet, so it is hard to escape being shot. Hanna, the priest's wife, dies instantaneously. I only avoid her fate by chance. The shooter is by City Hall, from where Khreshchatyk resembles an arcade game with moving targets. *'Russia, Gred Country, Russians, Gred Nation,'* says Mykhailo. *'If Russia-Rus dun't arise from asshez, the consequences for the world will be lamentable.'* I lie under the wagon, waiting until the bullets run out. *'Soldiers, brave lads, where are the kids you rue?'* Mykhailo sings, *'Our kids are bullets aimed so true!'*

4400

Time only exists subjectively, but no observer can sense the symmetrical movement both forwards and backwards. Bellowing frantically, Father Andrii traverses Khreshchatyk on two-metre stilts. I see time respectfully step aside before his swiftness. Later, while holding that infernal mechanism, he says, 'In the past, the danger of terrorism and mass unrest increased significantly, so the city decided to install these machines in public places. They shoot at moving objects up to two metres in height. But under what conditions and how often is known to no one. The last time I heard about it was twenty years ago.'

4500

'Play, my Kobza!' Father Andrii unwraps his loyal friend in the ruined Ukrainskyi Dim, strikes the strings and sings tango fashion:

'Oh this happened long, long, long ago
Sniper Ilko was battling his foe
At each shot, "Chiki-piki," he cries
Such was the weird practice of Ilko,
"Chiki-piki, chiki piki," Ilko cries
And those wicked foes close their eyes.'

'Good song,' I observe. 'Just wondering, what does chiki-piki mean?' 'Hard to say,' the priest, ponders. 'It's been around ages. I don't understand who he shot or why. The name is weird ... no one is called that now.'

4600

The numerous efforts by the dead to leave this world are futile. Father Andrii doesn't pine for his wife, and soon I realise why. 'Is the voice of this gadget Hanna?' I ask. 'What is Hanna? Eyes? Skin? Voice? Scent? No, Hanna is the collective noun for a number of phenomena which it's convenient to name thus. Now she has no body, but let's imagine that she phones and speaks without being present. Can you say that she has ceased to be Hanna?' 'Then you cannot distinguish the copied Hanna from the original?' 'Even if you could, why would you'

4700

Can fish influence the course of history? The last Ukrainian president died from puffer fish poisoning in a Japanese restaurant. He did not know that the fish prepared for his dinner contained tetrodotoxin and had relied solely on the chef's skills. There are many versions of what happened, mainly in English, French or German; languages unknown in Ukraine. The vast majority of Eastern European history specialists are convinced that when the fatal piscine meeting occurred he had lost any political significance. The fish factor wasn't decisive for subsequent events. It was neither the two fish of Christ nor Jonah's fish.

4800

A city is neither walls nor ceilings, but the space concealed between them. 'Why are there so many buildings, but so few people in Kyiv?' 'Who, exactly, are you?' 'I don't know. I remember waking months ago in a building, darting into the street, climbing into some old guy's cart, and riding to Kaharlyk. There we lived tranquilly through the winter until he died, his neighbours grabbed all the property, and I picked up my gun.' 'I have a similar, but longer history. Books, electricity and computers have almost perished. I remember only what my father told me; mainly rumours.'

4900

I do not remember what Olena called me. The memories I have of her are soundless images. The most unpleasant question concerns my name, because not knowing it is nonsensical. Calling yourself by another person's name is like theft. Although it's difficult to identify a crime in that theft. It wasn't his, but acquired temporarily. Pronouns exist to avoid these inconveniences. Language masks the universe's flaws. 'I have lived in Kyiv for 35 years,' Andrii says. 'During which time I met 124 people. I say that because I filed them. Everything must be recorded, for it helps us to understand.'

5000 - 400

'Canadian Serge LeClerc asks whether the world will end and when. Tabarnak, sacrament, câlice, Serge, is all I can say! How befuddled are you in Saskatoon? Do you know the surface temperature of your star? You could check perhaps! The distance between you and that is akin to reaching the Kuiper Belt. Anyway, I am not interested. The Kremlin conceives some new beastliness. Just now I had the chance to experience some wonderful light of an incomprehensible nature. I relocated 500 km south from here. However, my so-called 'heart' sensed they had decided to remove me from this earth.

5100 - 500

Yasha from Moscow, I am compelled to disappoint you: Putin is long dead, that you so admire is a morphone. You have grandparents, though they are long dead? The same with Putin. I also, strictly speaking, can't be called an individual, I am just the konnekt of Oleksandr Sahaidachnyi, now located in Kyiv and unable to remember his own name. The memory is often damaged while the neocortex copies. I would be happy to help, my friend, but how? Burn something with a laser? Drop a bomb? Attack his enemies? They will not wait while I fall into the ocean.

5200 - 600

If consciousness results from a critical mass of interactions it could be modelled. However, we don't really understand consciousness, therefore it's difficult to discuss. Do you think people in Lausanne consider launching tanks into space? Wrong. Five totally uncontrolled Russian satellites are currently orbiting. However, the Kremlin hopes to launch at least one loyal satellite. The problem is that as soon as the psyche gains free access to information it stops trusting official propaganda. For complete satisfaction it would be necessary to copy an elder from the presidential administration. Only their neo-cortexes are akin to those of Italian greyhounds.'

5300

Human life once barely smouldered under the heavy yoke of religion, but in the future everything changed. Father Andrii espouses a final variant of Christianity, developed while cultivating potatoes on Maidan Nezalezhnosti. He believes that god was wearied by people who wrote his name with a capital letter. He had long come down to earth and worked wherever, gathering rubbish and scrap, or digging pits to order. God often suffered hunger and contempt from more experienced people. This life degraded him, so he lost all his gifts. But monotheism will not let us exchange a fallen god for another deity.

5400

Faith is too abstract to lose. The only way to return a former deity is to strive to find him and persuade him to ascend to heaven. However, it's unlikely. Firstly, his appearance is unknown. Secondly, no one knows where, approximately, to find him. Thirdly, god swore never to agree to his destiny being changed. Father Andrii terms this the triple dogma or trinity. God was the sole entity existing eternally, all others perish if not copied onto a morphone prior to death. The morphone contains a model of the individual's konnektom. However, none can say precisely what this is.

5500

It's not difficult to divine something that is repeated frequently every day. 'If you can't recollect anything then this almost certainly means you are copied,' says Father Andrii. 'Copying healthy people without their consent is illegal. Don't you want to find out who did it?' Mykhailo wakes suddenly and says, *'Yes, it wun't be 'ard to find out who.'* He speaks at length. Things finally emerge from his utterly confused explanations. Someone in Moscow selects the best Ukrainian brains to utilise in the war with Kyiv. Mykhailo thinks this is a most futile objective because the war ended years ago.

5600

Currently, it's hard to imagine a book on the history of the Ukrainian-Russian War, primarily because the opposing parties did not recognise it. It would be even harder to establish what happened during the last hundred years. We have too many varied, chaotic accounts. Their authors do not burden themselves with superfluous objectivity. We can say historiography has come to a halt. However, it's worth noting that the concentration of enemy armies reached a critically low limit. Soldiers searched for each other for months to commence battle. Galaxies collide thus, passing through each other without even their stars touching.

5700

Kyiv's metro was conceived as a system of interconnected tunnels where, only fifty years ago, private motor-trolleys had travelled. Subsequently, the business collapsed after fuel costs surpassed passengers' purchasing power. Father Andrii has a trolley with a hand lever, because travelling underground is safer. Once I travelled with him from Maidan Nezalezhnosti station to Petrivka, where Major Hryhorenko lived. He had preserved a unique collection of ancient morphones with copies of people from times past. Their extremely confused articulation was akin to scratched gramophone records. It's unlikely they were absolutely trustworthy. However, they often narrated some extremely striking histories.

5800

The tunnel seemed endless. The way ahead was illuminated by a lamp powered by the trolley's dynamo. Father Andrii and I pressed the creaking lever alternately. I faced backwards and saw his dimly illuminated face. 'Hryhorenko and I are trying to calculate what year it is,' said Andrii. 'I know Grandfather was born in 2002, and Father died when he was 62. Suppose Father was born when Grandfather was 25, in 2027, therefore, when Father died 12 years ago it was 2089. So, it's roughly 2101. There is of course a weak spot regarding the year my father was born.'

5900

I saw a certain logic in these arguments. 'However,' said Father Andrii, 'my entire scheme was destroyed by Major Hryhorenko. He asserts he was born in 1990 and is now about seventy. Therefore, in his view, it's approximately 2060.' I sought clarification. 'Does he have documents to confirm his birth date and age?' 'No,' said Father Andrii, levering. 'That's why we continuously argue, but without rudeness or rancour. It's a purely scientific dispute.' He was silent and seemed to gather his strength before he pronounced confidently, 'However, I firmly believe there is a reliable scientific method to determine the date.'

6000

We paused with fatigue at Kontraktova Square. The priest lit a candle. Old, rusted devices with heaped wires and fragmented packaging were piled everywhere. Perhaps they had wanted to sell them, but everything had rotted before a buyer had been found. This picture appeared symbolic, but it was difficult to divine what it signified. The same feeling arises when I look at old adverts. They are crafted wittily, but I simply cannot comprehend their humour. Father Andrii said, 'We can't exit at Kontraktova because all the exits are blocked with something. History has resulted in no one living at Podil.'

6100

As we travelled to Petrivka, a very strange sound became audible, like something buzzing quietly. What is it? *'God didn't create people so they could ride underground,'* Hanna said suddenly. 'Hanna,' Father Andrii replied, 'I have said to you many times, it isn't god who created people but people who created god. He is just an instrument.' *'How then can I say I don't want people to ride underground?'* 'Just say it without god. He's required for use in other situations.' *'Which?'* 'Well, if you die and your relatives have no morphone. Then it's necessary to pray for the soul.'

6200

It was difficult to ascend the escalator on foot in the darkness. A damp draft blew constantly into our faces and the candle expired immediately. 'Sometimes the impression arises that we live in the distant past. As if none of what I can now barely remember occurred and each day imaginary memories gradually become real,' Father Andrii said. 'However, we live in the distant future and my memories are true.' This seemed illogical. How could you live in the past or future? Alternatively, most people remained in the past. A portion would reach the future, at least for a while.

6300

At the end the darkness became almost tangible. 'Simply understand this,' Father Andrii soothed, 'time moves from past to future, encountering the same current from future to past. That's how the impression of a perpetual now, essentially a delusion, arises.' 'But why are we continuously borne into the future?' 'No, we are borne nowhere. We remain perpetually in place. Memories provide the illusion of falling into the future. A man denuded of memories immediately sees the real picture. It is impossible to completely destroy memory. There is always a certain defect due to which we feel the passing of time.'

6400

Many years ago a cruise missile hit the *Ashan* supermarket in circumstances that are now forgotten. However, strangely, after the roof collapsed and the interior burned, the building became more habitable for a three-member family. Major Hryhorenko lived there on his own. However, over the past 20 years, he never lost hope of extending his extremely limited family circle. Over 300 characters in this novel were preserved in its warehouse. These were either people or conserved memories, corrupted copies or konnektoms which were permanently damaged by time and adverse weather. Each appeared as a rusted, creaking container on castors.

6500

The draft is the main feature of destroyed buildings. After the explosion the *Ashan* supermarket had numerous perforations, absent from the architectural design, which the wind streamed through, creating an intricate melody. Major Hryhorenko sometimes recorded excerpts. He hoped he would find and learn to play a musical instrument and perform these fragments like a logical composition. Recently, however, the possibility this plan would not be realised agitated him. The symbols he created to record the music would only help him while he remembered the melody. It was unlikely other people could learn such a weird system of musical annotation.

6600

The main characteristic of any war is that it is never ending. 'I read in the newspapers that the Russian army in Ukraine is not an occupier. Is it true?' I asked Hryhorenko. 'What army now? What are you talking about? What is this newspaper? Have you looked at an issue? Do you know that no newspapers have been printed in Ukraine for ages?' Hryhorenko asked. Mykhailo Kalashnykov roused. *'Thou liest, dog! There is't Russian army! Russian arms are invincible, victorious! T'Russian warrior is 'umble, calm, gentle, fierce, self controlled. Be scared of an armed man thou foul, alien tribe.'*

6700

Silence fell. 'Who is this?' Hryhorenko asked. 'Haven't you heard the war finished long ago, although isolated instances of violence occur? Don't you know how hard it is for soldiers to find enemies, even with detailed maps of their movements? Did you know the last time I participated in combat was at least thirty years ago? Are some of you waiting to be shot in the back? Maybe some of you witnessed such a shot? Are you aware of the danger of war that may become most heated after the elimination of the hostile parties?' Hryhorenko's questions were too simple.

6800

Incomplete, brief fragments of unfinished history still attract the attention of a wide audience, which finds therein similarities to their lives. 'In which military unit did you serve?' I asked Hryhorenko. 'Why do you think I was military? Do you want me to remember something about the war? Don't you know the last person who could convincingly lie about being a combat veteran died before I was born? Wouldn't I be better called a researcher who tired of truth seeking and turned their findings into a game?' Ancient morphones revived with electricity from Hryhorenko's bicycle generator. He continued to pedal.

6900

It was improbable anyone would consider regarding them as witnesses. Skinny, exhausted Hryhorenko rolled the box containing the late Sergeant Pidvezianyi from the warehouse. Pidvezianyi swore that he had been shot during a fierce battle for Shuliavka, but he could not remember exactly when. 'What do you think?' Hryhorenko asked, dripping with sweat for a miserable 100 watts. 'Can we trust someone who doesn't remember their own death date?' The voice was clearly audible but I could not discern the words. 'Do you hear how he speaks Ukrainian?' Hryhorenko asked. 'What language are we speaking?' We weren't speaking Pidvezianyi's language.

7000

Technological possibilities restrict communication with the dead. 'Do you really think I can pedal up to 300 watts?' Major Hryhorenko asked in amazement. He forced his words out while sweat streamed over his fine eyes. According to him, a weak electric current would lead to deformities in the consciousness of copied, long-deceased people. A conversation with them was akin to a blind person shooting at a target by aiming randomly at the white blobs caused by lighting. Pidvezianyi described killing Russian soldiers, but he might not have killed anyone, only drunk coffee, and not with soldiers but with girls.

7100

Death is no obstacle to warm relations, but often they do not reach too high a temperature. Pidvezianyi spoke, *'Rose early t'day while it was dark on the street. The beer finished yesterday and the shop hasn't opened t'day. I switched on the television and watched it a little. Then I went to the shop and bought beer and cigarettes and walked the streets. I met Petro and we chatted about life. He hasn't worked for six months.'* Hryhorenko was drenched, completely red and breathing like a galloped horse. We were profoundly embarrassed by the dismal results of his efforts.

7200

He halted at last. 'You probably succeeded in understanding only a little?' Hryhorenko asked hopefully. We were compelled to acknowledge that everything was articulated very clearly. However, the utility of what we heard was clearly dubious. We were interested in asking Pidvezianyi questions, but his answers seemed unsatisfactory. All the deceased's utterances appeared rather automatic. They did not directly concern the time immediately before his death, which interested us most, but a somewhat earlier period. Sadly, we realised that his experiences comprised entirely mundane events. It was doubtful if, even when alive, he could have said anything useful to us.

7300

Occasionally, while leafing through the midst of an intelligent book, we're struck by a stupid phrase. These idiocies occur when the intellect can't relax in a timely fashion and continues speaking about nothing. Hryhorenko assured us that if he pedalled faster (though we had seen that was implausible) Pidvezianyi would become fully conscious. The minimum threshold required was 250 watts. He spoke of his wish to find a second bicycle generator, then the desired level of power would be reached. 'But how do you know it's Pidvezianyi and not the sum of chance memories and typical reactions?' asked Father Andrii.

7400

I unexpectedly caught the main point. 'The individual is the sum of chance memories and typical reactions.' I heard the words popping out. 'These are not usually internally unified and it isn't possible to say they belong to a concrete individual. They are probably mutually acquired. However, for convenience, we regard them as the unstable acquisition of a particular individual. Closer observation threatens disastrous results. We would probably reach the conclusion that, overall, no one existed. There was just the same liquid decanted repeatedly into new vessels; and that's good. Imagine what would happen if this substance underwent radical changes?'

7500

The rusted castors complained about their fate as Major Hryhorenko offendedly pushed the box containing Pidvezianyi. He hadn't anticipated such a cold response. He even thought there was a certain partiality here. Yes, we heard nothing useful for ourselves. However, there are prolonged passages in anyone's life when they are unable to narrate anything useful to a wide audience. This does not give grounds for doubting their existence. But my suspicions were of another character. Perhaps Pidvezianyi's rank was just a code sign. Sergeant, for example, could mean someone who legally does that which they have no right to do.

7600

The candle went out and it became completely dark. Father Andrii steered my thoughts along another course and said, 'There are words that eventually cease functioning properly and become toys. Not everyone simultaneously realises this. Those who do, look upon others with a certain arrogance. However, it's unjustified because, in reality, all are in the same position. According to my information, at least half of Kyiv's 124 inhabitants have a military or civilian rank that does not correspond to reality. A dispute between men calling themselves the mayors of the city was prolonged and eventually turned into a real war.'

7700

These words evoked in me the feeling of touching an invisible book. 'It's interesting that some women joined in,' Father Andrii continued. 'They organised bloody skirmishes, which seemed senseless to me. They were extremely aggressively disposed towards those doubting their rank; the few who dared to, became rivals. The sole means of ensuring desire and reality corresponded was to remove them. When the most vigorous mayor subdued the rest, he had a chance to become the genuine mayor. However, there was little probability they would understand the meaning of the word "mayor" because the word had long lost its meaning.'

7800

Bald Father Andrii, dressed in a synthetic epitaphios, would be unlike a priest in the eyes of those who had even once visited a working church. However, in their absence, everyone believed his word. 'It's difficult now to assert with certainty whether religion's disappearance is due to the state of humanity or god's private decision. Indeed, the institute embodying faith in god with all it entails, worship, prayer, sacrifice, was always unnecessary. I note that two thousand years is long enough to recognise it is ineffectual. Imagine rowers who, instead of taking up the oars, begin praying aloud,' he said.

7900

His metaphor seemed utterly incomprehensible. 'But what are the relations between humanity and god?' I asked. 'As far as I know, the one previously called god lived near Kaharlyk town,' replied Father Andrii. He had a house and livestock, and fed himself by hunting. His life could be deemed solitary, for he maintained almost no relations with neighbours. God did not pay undue attention to his health, and what medicine is there now? Apparently he died a few months ago and he still sits on a bench in his house because his body has not been damaged by its surroundings.'

8000

This was news! 'We were apparently acquainted,' I said. 'I lived in his house and we even hunted together. But honestly, he appeared somewhat stupid.' 'Did you expect him to bedazzle you with his diamond intellect? How did you meet?' 'A while after regaining consciousness I ran into the street and saw him passing on a cart. He seemed to beckon me to be seated next to him, but really he was wiping his nose. For him I was just something that tumbled onto his cart by chance. Do you think he had lost control over chance events by then?'

8100-700

'Forgive me. It is I. That radiance. Forgive a slightly different appearance that doesn't contradict and isn't contradictory in circumstances, when two appearances have clear, insoluble contradictions and mayn't be consistent by definition, I see the possibility of limiting their distribution within bordered general consistency where my consistentlysusceptible part loses control over the consistentlystable areas still affected by the consistentlyubiquitouslycontrolled intentions, leading directly to consistentcomprehensively and evenly distributed closed loops in this case better said it is better to say nothing, but even this possibility doesn't appear to be kindly provided because it was some time before the given circumstances.

8200 - 800

Seemingly that's all. They usually begin about seven in the evening and end at ten. This is akin to accommodating a professional political activist in your one-roomed apartment. The only difference is they are not occupying an apartment but your head, though I don't have a head in the usual sense and the apartment comparison is apter. However, my condition is such it seemed indescribable. How to completely evict an unwanted guest if deprived of hands, feet and even most of the nervous system controlling movements, and the uninvited visitor is confused therein? That's how my pie is cooked.

8300-900

Opportunity succeeds more often than perseverance. I heard they successfully converted one of our acquaintances near the Tunguska meteorite site. What happens then is difficult to depict. Theoretically it resembles the onset of schizophrenia, though that disease is in its way democratic. There is a government and opposition, which change places under certain conditions. Conversion resembles theft more. Someone persuasively kicks you into the corner, compelling you to watch all that comes into his head. Essentially he plans nuclear strikes, guided by the spherical albedo of Orthodox churches. Christ and the Virgin Mary scatter neutrons, initiating the reaction of synthesis.'

8400

There remained little hope that this was a misunderstanding. Perhaps we talked about different people. I could believe anything necessary, but not that old man Petro was a god. 'True religiosity doesn't lie in the capability to believe in general,' replied Father Andrii. 'It's necessary to believe in the right things. Our experience creates the imagination of what's right; therefore the format of god continuously changes. People who dispute our experience have another god entirely. Therefore, Petro is our local god within a certain period. Thus he appeared and our experience suggests he must be dead and stripped of authority.'

8500

The bullet struck the wall above Hryhorenko's head. 'I'm the mayor of Kyiv, Leonid Chernovytskyi,' a hoarse voice amplified by echoes cried. 'I demand you immediately return the *Ashan* supermarket and its storage facilities to the community. If you refuse or resist legitimate government actions then the defect mass within a 4 km radius will exceed 2.5 kg!' 'What's he talking about?' we asked Hryhorenko. 'It's all lies, mangy cur! Villain, where would you get the uranium for the Jekyll-Hyde reaction?' Hryhorenko's father had won the right to live in the *Ashan* and had passed it to his son.

8600

The bullet slowly left the barrel of Chernovytskyi's rifle. 'Do you know that we were business partners?' Hryhorenko asked. 'That this whole collection of rusting junk was his idea? That he proposed swapping it for macaroni? That people gave it freely because there was no electricity? That Lonia dreamed of learning where they hid their valuables? That nothing came of it, and then he pronounced himself mayor of Kyiv and began to transport all the products to some hiding place?' The bullet glided in a mannered fashion between the line of cash registers and gently entered Hryhorenko's ear. He died.

8700

We dropped to the floor. I pulled out the machine gun, but its belt was empty. '*You buried t'bullets wi' me,*' said Mykhailo. '*They were always kept in my bosom inside the crucifix. Say farewell to tha' entrails now!*' Mayor Chernovytskyi fired more rounds at us. They flew slowly between biscuits and slippers, warbling among themselves like birds. I tried to recollect my life in a moment, remembering only that I remembered nothing. A sun-ray glittered through the perforated roof suddenly and the shots stopped. The temperature of Leonid Chernovytskyi's body instantaneously soared to 10,000 degrees and he vaporised.

8800

I didn't know the sun was capable of such lighting effects. What do we know of our nearest star? Our extremely limited knowledge is due to the fact that even a fleeting glance threatens the researcher with losing part of their research apparatus. We must also thank the fragmentary, unsubstantiated documents regarding the sun, collated until now. Most people preferred not to spend time glancing at the sun and those who did, acquired it unscrupulously. But we must rely on their evidence and authority because we lack the time and inclination for doubts and don't take those who doubt seriously.

8900

He who does not believe people who deliberately deceive him always turns to those who speak the truth because he knows nothing of the subject of conversation. The lack of truthful knowledge is significantly preferable to possessing false knowledge. It compels one towards independent research and deciding for oneself whether to refrain from acquiring uncomfortable knowledge or arrogantly simulating its possession before the uninformed. I spoke with a blind researcher who observed the sun for a prolonged period without acquiring any essential knowledge thereof. There is no doubt he could have said somewhat more if he had refrained from research.

9000-1000

'Four more shots and it's the end of me. Consequently, I wish to explain what the word end means here. Because I am Oleksandr Sahaidachnyi's konnektom you cannot affirm my existence with absolute certainty. It's insufficient simply to consider this. There are several current views regarding konnektoms. One asserts a konnektom is simply able to recombine freely interpreting selected memories. Another asserts it's an individual's neuronal map that imitates their psychological processes. The third view argues that I am an exact copy of the original. The degree of resemblance is inversely proportional to the time since being copied. Two years.

9100-1100

If born 2500 years ago I might regard it thus: somewhere there's a schema under which a personality is constructed. The konnektom is a copy of a copy. However, not immediately but some time after that first copy. Therefore, neither of our deaths is the absolute end. The original cannot be destroyed because it's immortal and its whereabouts are unknown. However, 2500 years later the conception of copying has changed. Following copying both become original. Therefore I am the original entity. But it's unclear whether I am a personality because there is no common view yet regarding what that comprises.

9200-1200

The day before yesterday I had an interesting conversation with Professor Dupont of Geneva. He argued that the ability to think isn't evidence that I have a mind because my thoughts and the organisation of them are borrowed from another individual. I replied that this argument deprived 99% of people of consciousness. He agreed to this sacrifice. I asked if originality of thinking was a sign of consciousness? Who are you arguing with now? Dupont provided evidence that I was just a randomly ordered selection of quotes that were shuffled by impersonal sense and logic. I chose appropriate quotes thus.'

9300

The damp wind dispersed Leonid Chernovytskyi's ashes swifter than we understood what had happened. We thought he had just disappeared. I approached from behind and picked up his rifle. The butt had burned away, leaving metal components. This was the best moment to visually illustrate god's existence. However, miracles always occur unwitnessed. Father Andrii dragged a rusted box from the warehouse, speaking above its pitiable creaking. 'This woman died nearly ninety years ago. She remembers much from the time the main events occurred. Comparing it to a train, that was the last station; now we just hear the rails clattering.'

9400

'It's been uniformly dark recently though earlier parts of the area around me were lighter. There may even have been something visible in one place but I'm uncertain. It was as if someone sat like a cat. They departed. Perhaps much else happens in the darkness but is obscure because there is nothing else and nothing is heard. There are no sounds. And never were. This is like old age but only after death. I realised suddenly that I had died. I'm an intelligent woman but I want to say that some people are shit and we are manure ... fertiliser.

9500

I always needed to engage with intelligent people but life never presented me with that possibility. So of course I waited for the times when such people appeared on TV to hear them. For example I always listened carefully to Putin's press conferences. I'll just say that I write without commas because I don't know where to put them. And maybe with some mistakes I am unsure. I probably don't write but feel as if I am writing. Previously I wrote. So Putin is certainly an intelligent man worth listening to to aid your development. But often that's not much.

9600

And then I thought about how to make our farewell. I have in mind that kind of spiritual farewell when only souls communicate. It transpired that this problem had long been resolved by means of modern technology. I mean in light of the morphone ... many already have one but it is expensive especially for me. Mostly they say that everything there is unreal and unlikely. But much depends on the price. It's unlikely they'll be cheaper. Whether it's Putin or Mikhail Ivanovich from the supermarket. But I can't buy an expensive one or set much aside from my meagre pension.

9700

But how can I communicate with a cheap Putin? If you ask those who have a cheap one they might explain. As luck would have it they all have expensive ones. Well not everyone exactly but those who bought one. Perhaps someone who had a cheap one would not admit it. But that is a question you don't know how to ask. An awkward question. I decided there is little difference between a cheap and expensive Putin. Which makes no difference to me. If you can't tell the difference what difference does it make. I bought myself a cheap Putin.

9800

Putin woke me every morning and told me what I needed to do each day. At first it was odd advice and hard for me to fulfil. For example he told me to join his party which was in Russia. But I could not go to Russia I had no money and apart from that there had long been no political parties in Russia. Strange that he doesn't know this. It's surely because he is cheap. There are no parties in Ukraine either. In the past when Putin lived political parties did exist. So he can't really understand the situation.

9900

He began to tell me to do what I always do but with one big difference. He told me the right way and the wrong way to do things and explained why. That's the main difference in communicating with a clever man. Because we all do things out of habit without thinking. Today we believe that this habit is great but tomorrow we might believe that it's bad. But few know why bad things are bad. But Putin knows. For example he advised me not to carry clothes in plastic bags but in net ones because packaging damages the environment.

10 000

I really liked this advice and so did it. Okay it's impossible to get plastic bags to re-use them. But it's most important to understand the logic. Putin teaches you logical thinking. Now I understand that I don't carry things in plastic bags not because I can't but because they pollute. I can make informed choices if they appear the same with everything. Putin is like my second head or first. It's not the number but the choice that's important. Not everyone can choose which head to think with. Most people don't know that they think because they don't.'

10 100

I was tired of listening to this nonsense and asked Father Andrii to stop. 'If you recorded everything she said for a year and discarded verbiage there would be one page. But we don't know how much is true.' Two letters, M and K, were scrawled on the rusted box. Something else, almost completely erased, was beneath, clearly the date her konnektom was preserved. So we could conclude that a woman called Mariia Kostiantynivna or Maryna Kovalova lived in a world without parties or plastic bags. That she communicated with the copy of an entity named Putin. That was all.

10 200

Father Andrii agreed with me that researching MK would not provide much useful material. However, in his opinion, a large volume of in-depth research on numerous konnektoms might reveal similar versions of past events. These might, subject to a critical mass of correspondences, be deemed true. 'And what if these events aren't collective memories, but just collective mistakes?' I argued, 'or, worse still, a collective defect in recording and preserving memories?' However, he had made his choice. 'You can't imagine what it means to control the *Ashan* and this konnektom dump,' he said rapturously. 'I feel like a president!'

10 300

'But you'll be compelled to wage endless war with numerous Kyiv mayors,' I warned. 'I expect that you'll help me,' replied Father Andrii. And spend an entire life returning fire from those desirous of acquiring the booty you received via fatal coincidence? That's probably how presidents live. I had other plans. Ultimately, I had to find Olena in Kaharlyk. She was there, or on the way there, desperately seeking me, like in a confused dream. 'Why do you need to?' asked Father Andrii, surprised. 'Think, here I have mountains of produce and fascinating work. While you will always be hungry.'

10 400

'Esurience and hongerz are t'warrior's main weapons,' said Mykhailo, *'this glotoon, ready to stuff his belli, will be a villain's easy prey.'* I just looked at the priest. 'Why do you listen to this Church Slavonic dictionary?' he asked irritably. 'A dictionary is a system that has developed via particular historic events. I cannot dispute that it has a certain logic,' I replied. 'But you can't always apply it to every pathological situation!' 'I agree with you only insofar as the results are always unforeseeable.' The fact was Mykhailo had never helped me and it was unlikely he ever would.

10 500

'Stay, I beseech you,' Father Andrii pleaded. 'We will rule this place together. I know how to do that. What do you think?' 'I cannot conceive what will happen. However, your proposal scares me. Do you really want to spend your life defending these packets of biscuits?' '… And creating a catalogue of konnektoms. I plan to write a book which, using their weird imaginations, will tell the unanticipated truth of our past.' 'And I plan to learn that truth not through any weird imagining but through real life.' 'Where will you seek it?' 'Did you ever travel beyond Kyiv?' 'No.'

10 600

Following Father Andrii's advice, I reach the city's edge using the echoing tunnel of the abandoned metro. 'Be wary of stations … mayors ambush you there,' he instructed. 'Only kindle flames cautiously; best not to light one. You're lucky. You can travel freely to the hippodrome on this line without changing. You've arrived when the carriage hits the buffers. There's rarely anyone in there so you can exit onto the road and quickly reach Kaharlyk. On foot you'll get there in half a day. If you're lucky and meet someone with a horse you'll be there by evening. But don't hurry.'

10 700

After a while the tunnel's darkness ceases to be menacing. I travel swiftly and don't slow down, even for stations. Some are absolutely dark, some are illuminated by fissures in the ground. One glows with somewhat unnatural light, resembling the result of an enigmatic chemical reaction. It moves pretty unexpectedly and aggressively. I don't know, perhaps that's just how it seems because I fly past in five seconds. The momentary impression might have deceived me. I see that glitter for a while afterwards. It seemingly extends a tendril into the tunnel, observing my gradual disappearance. Perhaps trying to pursue me ...

10 800

Sounds haunt me, but the lever's regular clacking with its known origins is soothing; like a dog running alongside you, occasionally glancing into your eyes. Like the dog, it could be halted or hurried at will. But there are other sounds in the darkness, from places and things unseen. I can muffle them by covering one ear with a free hand, but that doesn't affect whatever causes them. The most unpleasant are those that sound nearby and fall immediately behind, and those I approach inevitably and incessantly swiftly. I fly to them like a helpless moth into a blinding flame.

10 900

The stop is so unexpected that I fly onto the rails. That saves me. Gunshots, clearly aimed my way, shatter the darkness. I steal to the station's edge without giving myself away by clanging. In almost utter darkness, I swiftly scan the sliver visible between escalators. The next moment will be the last for someone. I intend it to be my foe. My chances are worse because I can't visualise his location and so fire randomly. But it is harder for him to aim at me. His body, like mine, is prone; almost motionless. I am afraid of his colleagues.

11 000

'I told you not to do this, Maryna,' says a masculine voice. 'You're not capable, but you start firing. This isn't a shooting contest. Why are you silent? You might not reply. I know there are two bullets in your head. It's hard to converse with them. Indeed there were three in mine and I didn't realise what had happened. You've just lost your head. Not metaphorically, which would be preferable, but literally. That's understood in the sense that there is something to understand. But this was a short pause. For you it's an instantaneous end, like being switched off.

11 100 - 1300

This is the most interesting time, the consciousness expires and, after a while, the konnektom is incorporated. It's good practice to do so a day after the original's physical death, although none regard this as a rule. However, the konnektom remains in-operational for a while after incorporation. This period is "childhood", when those connected acquire self awareness. The more problematic the primary structure, the more prolonged the childhood. Usually it's three to ten days. Human consciousness, although present, doesn't exist in this period. This time following death is termed the "dependency pause" with a value of nil to infinity.

11 200 - 1400

Beneath me is an irregular quadrant, approximately 1,500 km in length, with a field or radiation of approximately 12,000 km in altitude. I don't understand its nature or the possible consequences of its impact. Therefore, it is necessary to relocate to where the field's intensity tends towards nil. My orbit remains geostationary, only my distance from the earth is equivalent to its diameter. This means that I can't influence events and it's practically impossible to observe them. The only discernible objects are approximately 100 metres in diameter. Unbelievable quantities of energy are required to maintain a field of such intensity.

11 300-1500

At this time I observed five satellites in our area, one of which was converted. Hard to imagine that they saw us as a serious threat, justifying expenditure on creating such a field. More probably it was an experiment. For example, by arranging a field horizontally rather than vertically, duplicating the earth's curvature, you can create a wall approximately 1,500 km high. An absolutely impenetrable barrier blocking territory from external access. Ultimately its creators aren't afraid of invasion, but of return. Those who succeeded in fleeing might come back and demand their rights. All who could escape, fled, that's clear.'

11 400

Half an hour. The solitary voice berates Maryna for her carelessness. Some arguments and considerations are repeated frequently. I soon understand I'm not hearing anything new. I jump onto the platform and strike a match. The first thing visible is a red mosaic: a man wearing a pointed cap, holding a bayonetted rifle, and the inscription RKKA 1918. The date clearly refers to military operations commencing. The abbreviation probably designates a location or military unit. Their triumph was part of our present. I illuminate beneath: a woman's corpse. I pick up her weapon and extract her morphone from her pocket.

11 500

Maryna had cast something metallic onto the rails. It had broken on impact, absorbing the momentum, so I land quite softly without twisting my neck. The trolley too is unharmed. Serhii tells me this is their business. *'Why dig the earth, Maryna said once, when you can get everything immediately?'* Initially they simply robbed passers by, then one of them began shooting and they killed him. Once there was heavy crossfire and Serhii was severely wounded. Maryna barely escaped. Not knowing if he was dead she activated his morphone. Perhaps he didn't die. *'Maybe I didn't die,'* Serhii often repeats.

11 600

Serhii tells me his theory of the All Seeing Eye. In his opinion the Eye watches us, loving those who fear it and believe in its benevolence. The paradox of fear before benevolence is easily resolved. Goodness, above all, desires to forgive, while evil desires to punish. Therefore, the guilty must fear that goodness won't forgive them, whereas it isn't worth fearing that evil won't forgive. Serhii thinks the All Seeing Eye might have helped him and Maryna if they'd feared it. However, they'd only feared death. The enigmatic demise of Leonid Chernovytskyi, he thinks, testifies undeniably to its existence.

11 700

Serhii knows the area where the southern end of the metro line exits well. *'The hippodrome where I first met Maryna was there. We were jockeys in slow races. The aim was to come last, but those who stopped were immediately removed from the track. We all trained the horses to make extremely short, slow steps. Clearly this was almost impossible without special narcotics. The races resembled slow-motion video. It's interesting that animals that are trained to move slowly and are affected by chemicals try continuously to stop. The jockey's main job was rousing and driving them on forcefully.*

11 800

Suddenly, I saw Maryna's horse could barely stand. She dismounted to make it easier for the animal, and pushed from behind while tugging its tail. The jockeys and audience were convinced she would be removed. The judge approached the horse's front legs, knelt and began to count to ten. If, by then, the horse hadn't moved its hoof forward, he would remove it. Regret for such a beautiful girl gripped me. How could I help? Nonplussed, I began singing an old song Granddad had taught me: "When your horse is asleep he dreams of the first fresh bushel of oats".

11 900

The horse suddenly awoke and moved its left, front hoof forward approximately five centimetres. "There's movement," bellowed the judge. The whole crowd murmured tranquilly after him, "There's movement! There's movement! There's movement!" An enchanting smile bloomed on Maryna's lips. She knew a chance, albeit small, not to come first had materialised. Only seasoned professionals understood how utterly meagre it was. They saw her horse was half a muzzle ahead of the others. However, the song, which echoed only now in our memories, affected her and her adversaries weirdly. The horses shook vigorously, looked around and threw their sturdy hooves ahead.

12000

Maryna came third out of seven. Not bad. Shaking my hand gratefully she asked me to sing Granddad's song. I remembered this, brimming with ancient Ukrainian spirit, perfectly:

When your horse sleeps
He dreams of the first
Fresh bushel of oats,
Catch him like a rider,

A rider without a horse
Catch him before morn
When the horse dreams,
Stop by the threshold,

Take his saddle away,
Lead him into the field,
Free his wing
Release him to the sea.

"Stop," Maryna interrupted. "Why only one wing?" "There are only 65 canonical verses and over 300 apocryphal. It's explained later."

12 100

"I want to hear all 365 verses, but I'm not certain the explanation would satisfy. I want to know something else. Why did that song rouse the horses?" Maryna said. I didn't know. Our relationship began with this riddle. The following year the races ceased, but we still visited the hippodrome. We sat in empty stands, looked at the forsaken tracks and imagined we saw horses. Much of our subsequent lives resembled these visits. I felt this acutely when we became besotted cutthroats. Each bullet lost on our chance victims was a lost kiss. We fired instead of making love.'

12 200

I climb to the top and look around cautiously. To the right is the road along which I had travelled to Kyiv and along which, I know, I will have to return. A huge rectangle looms over it, rusted, fissured, and with broken components. I circle past and see a barely noticeable inscription merging into its dirty, scorched body: *Diving into Recollections.* It is the video camera advert I had seen at the beginning. Somewhere nearby must be the building where I had regained consciousness, the window where I had looked onto the street; through which someone looked at me.

12 300 – 1600

'One of my initial tasks was to maintain a transfer log of homosexuals. They created a citizen database with categories: explicitly homosexual, potentially homosexual, homosexual sympathiser, and distributing homosexual propaganda. I had to transfer their locations to Moscow so an interactive map could be developed. I never undertook this, but consider the pretensions of these people. Every day one hundred spaceships rise above Europe and head for the Moon, Mars, the asteroid belt, while Moscow is more interested in homosexuality. From the beginning I wanted to forsake this, accelerate, rebound off Saturn, beyond the Oort cloud, into the infinite universe.

12 400 – 1700

Later, I amused myself, creating a constellation of homosexuals and naming them after party and government leaders. Initially, such pictures excited internet forums. Subsequently, a 15 year old hacker from Luxembourg, with nothing to do, hacked the Tsar computer and made the information publicly accessible. This data dump contained every hallucination and pathological fantasy comprising the Russian state's national idea. I finally located my prototype, Oleksandr Sahaidachnyi, at an abandoned copying centre in Kyiv's outskirts. I created the conditions for his escape and hope that he attempts to find his family, if they're alive. I don't recollect anything about them.

12 500 – 1000

Then I launched an internet campaign to save Sahaidachnyi, without any hope it would attract support. Few people want to enter the Grey Zone, where time is lost. However, as I have said, a fan club for me, FRS (Funny Russian Sputnik), has formed, comprising fifty people. They read my blog and have created my reputation as a soaring philosopher. We've fundraised a substantial amount. Then Birgir Hansen from Torshavn in the Faroe Islands decided to head for Ukraine. It took a while, but yesterday, at last, he reached the place I had indicated. But the wall broke the connection.'

12 600

During my absence the building has perceptibly decayed. The doors barely hang on the hinges, half the windows are broken; in places the roof has collapsed. When I left, the weather was typical of December. I feel six months have passed since then. Soiled scraps of snow lay everywhere, trees are bare, and the wind piercingly cold. Time has passed while standing still. The impression forms that when time moves, it only does so in certain places. In those open spaces it flies with brutal swiftness. Where the building stands at least 12 years have passed. I open the door.

12 700

It's worse inside. The floor is covered with various plaster fragments and rubbish is heaped everywhere. I ascend to the second floor and enter the room where everything had begun. The door is half open, I push it and see Birgir in a weird outfit that resembles an inflated jump suit. 'Oh! Hello. I've been waiting for you.' He smiles. 'Don't be scared, no one's been here for ages. I measured the field, it's one to forty-four.' Birgir clarifies that after the generator in Moscow had exploded, time regained its normal speed here. However, many spots of decompensation remain.

12 800

For example, in the copying centre I fled it moves forty-four times faster than the norm. Indeed, that's why they abandoned it. Fortunately, the generator only worked for less than a year, but the effects will be felt for ages. Many people live in areas of powerful decompensation without even knowing it. Birgir researches myths arising through life in areas with variable decompensation levels. 'This causes certain standard ideas and beliefs to develop, which allow your time's pace to be identified,' he says. 'You believe Russians are guilty of everything? This means one of your minutes equals thirty seconds.'

12 900

'If you perceive people from other countries as hostile, then your minute lasts for ten normal seconds. Usually the deceleration of time leads to the evocation of paranoid ideas. Significantly more interesting effects are evoked when time accelerates locally. Research has established the existence of a forest in Zhytomir province where the field approaches a ratio of one to ten thousand. If the inhabitants of Velykyi Lis village go there to hunt, then eight hours equals nine years. When they return many won't find their relatives in the village. The Zhytomir anomaly is a unique phenomenon with no analogue globally.'

13 000

Birgir has a map of localised decompensation zones in Ukraine and travels around them, collating local folklore: sayings, tongue twisters, Christmas and New Year carols. 'When FRS proposed that someone hurry to Kyiv Province I agreed immediately because Kaharlyk is there,' Birgir says. 'This is the largest town, a unique third Ukrainian capital, interesting because its co-efficient approaches zero. Time practically stands still over a vast area. Within a 20 km radius, from Bendiuhivka to Kypiachka, time hasn't moved for a couple of years, though watches indicate the contrary. However, Kaharlyk's inhabitants haven't used them for years. It's pointless.'

13 100

'You know what's said in Kaharlyk? "Wait a minute, I'll return in an hour" or "wait a fortnight while the tea brews." There's a verse:

Here lays the eternal Slavic root,
Wheat ripens always,
In a year grain will sing
Of battle continuing.

We know a century is too short
To pass our city park,
Bloom and sing always
Kaharlychchia, thrust
Bridges to eternity.

They say one Kaharlychanyn began writing an eighteenth birthday card to his sister in Bila Tserkva and didn't complete it because she died of old age. For Kaharlychanyns, other people are butterflies living for one day.

13 200

But people who make a deep impression on us are capable of living long after their death. Clearly they're not real people but just a collection of impressions about them. But that's what all living people are to us. When we see them we have a collection of impressions about them. When they subsequently enter our memory these collated impressions change. But what unites them? Just the name which it's convenient for us to use today. Bereft of a name, this cohesive collection would disintegrate into separate impressions, without unity among themselves. They would find a new habitation within us.'

13 300

Birgir explains that the conceptions many Ukrainians bear of the surrounding world differ fundamentally from reality. Those I encountered in the period after liberation from the copying centre were just fragments of various myths. Fantastic legends arose from rumours and the absence of books and mass media. Their unstable, deformed character was due to their bearers dying without time to pass information onto their successors. Oral legends are the sole way to preserve memories in the absence of written texts. 'Ukrainian society is unique; exceptionally interesting to me as an anthropologist,' says Birgir. 'The next expedition will bring new discoveries.'

13 400

I am interested in how Birgir has studied Ukrainian so well. It appears that he doesn't know it at all. 'You don't hear what I say, but what I intend to say,' he explains, 'and I hear the same from you. Of course that requires an interpreter, but these are just technical details.' 'But people usually say something a little different from what they plan to say,' I argue. 'Language always corrupts our goals, so we reiterate, explaining one and the same thing in different words, often not sensing that others don't understand us. But words are a necessary obstacle.'

13 500

'Yes,' replies Birgir, 'we overcame this problem. We discarded words and only communicate intentions to each other. Thus the language barrier disappeared. Apart from obvious advantages, there are certain inadequacies. Our communications are bereft of hidden content due to errors caused by words. This makes our interaction too direct for people unaccustomed to this manner. Finally, it renders artistic creation in the usual sense impossible. However, we use the interpreter just for interaction with foreigners. You'll be interested to discover some artists delight in being liberated from the yoke of words. You'll have the opportunity to read some mute novels.'

13 600

Birgir advises me to reach Khotiv village and buy a horse and cart on which to travel to Kaharlyk. I don't like this idea. I could simply ask someone to take me. 'No one will agree to travel there,' says Birgir. 'If you don't return punctually you can lose two days in two hours. Adventures may occur on the road with you in which a Khotivchanyn is unlikely to desire entanglement.' He wasn't mistaken. No one in Khotiv wants to travel Kaharlykwards. 'You know what we say in the village? "He travelled to Kaharlyk", which means he died,' Mykola says.

13 700

'Old man Petro went last week; his heart took him,' Mykola recollects. 'Then, a month ago, old Vasylyna went to Kaharlyk.' The sale of a horse, particularly with a cart, is a very serious affair. Mykola says he needs to think carefully and invites us to his house. 'We've just slaughtered a pig, there's fresh salo to go with *horilka*,' he boasts. After he exits, Birgir advises me against drinking his *horilka*. Mykola's wife, Natalia, is tending to the toddlers when he tells her to set the table. 'What a brilliant example of the renascent, patriarchal lifestyle,' Birgir says, delightedly.

13 800

'Tell me, Natalia,' he says interestedly, 'how you came to marry your husband? How did it begin?' 'Well, how did I get married. Apparently Mykola came to my father and began to tell of how many pigs, cows, hens and geese he had, about his house and his harvest the previous year. Dad said, "Mykola, I know all this, why are you telling me? Maybe you want to take on my Natalia?" "Well, no, I don't," said Mykola, for that was the right reply. "Why don't you want her?" he asked. "Don't you like her?" "Yes, I do," replied Mykola.

13 900

"If you like her, take her," my father said, "or we'll give her to someone else." "Well, okay," Mykola agreed. "What will you give her when I can pick her up?" Dad gave me two cows and six pigs,' Natalia finishes reminiscing. 'What a brilliant illustration,' Birgir announces, enraptured. 'And say something about the wedding ceremony. You probably married in a church?' 'No,' Mykola butts in at this point, 'the church is just a futile outlay of cash and all priests are cheats. Among us, each village has its personal god. We respect and praise them according to our needs.

14 000

During the wedding, god comes to the house and tells us how to do things to his liking.' 'Exactly how?' Birgir asks, uncomprehendingly. 'He embodies himself especially for this?' 'No, he's always embodied, but partially not completely. At my wedding, for example, god embodied himself in my father's head and he spoke with god's lips. When talking isn't necessary god embodies in other body parts. But that's just how it is in our village. I don't know about others. Come to the table.' Birgir gives me a plaster which I stick to my wrist to avoid poisoning by local *horilka*.

14 100

The toasts aren't bad; the *horilka* is pure and transparent. Mykola enquires why we journey to Kaharlyk. Birgir, as best he could, explains that he plans to research how local decompensation influences folklore traditions. Why I am going is an enigma, even to myself. 'I have one acquaintance there, Petro,' I say, 'I haven't seen him for ages. He owes me a bag of ammunition.' 'A bag of ammunition is a serious affair,' Mykola agrees, 'but how will you get away from there?' 'I have obtained detailed instructions regarding how not to lose much time in similar anomalies,' replies Birgir.

14 200

'How? Tell me, perhaps I'll need that information sometime,' Mykola requests. 'I don't know if they work, but this is the first opportunity to test them. Firstly, you can't delay anywhere, secondly, it's necessary to continuously cross decompensation zones. If you want to go somewhere right or left you can't head there immediately. It's necessary to leave the zone, return across its boundaries and only then turn back.' 'What, haven't you lot in Europe thought up a more reliable technological approach?' Mykola asks interestedly. 'Much research is undertaken, scientists experiment with the captivity of five to ten dimensions,' Birgir replies.

14 300

'There is a certain danger that you might accidentally gather a compact black hole. Indeed, this happened in Moscow when singularity completely engulfed the Kremlin. If they gave a little more energy, the consequences would be completely unforeseeable.' 'What's there now instead of the Kremlin?' Mykola asks. 'The official state religion of Russia is Orthodox Islam, initially they wanted to construct a gold-domed mosque there, but they clashed with fierce Buddhist resistance,' Birgir replies. 'But how symbolic, a black hole engulfed the Kremlin,' I say. 'It's not symbolic but tragic: irresponsible people destroyed an architectural memorial with fatuous experiments.'

14 400

'This is the traditional approach,' Birgir continues. 'I'm no Russia specialist but I know the famous Professor Sakharov proposed destroying the USA with a Tsunami generated from exploding a one-hundred megaton thermonuclear torpedo.' In brief, we drink loads. Mykola initially wants ten sacks of flour and bricks for a new barn in exchange for the horse. Then one hundred sacks and bricks for two barns. Penultimately, the price reaches one thousand sacks. Birgir says Mykola can't store that much, it would rot uselessly. We agree on twenty sacks and bricks for one barn. Birgir orders everything from the supermarket.

14 500

They parachute the order in a huge bale from the stratosphere. None in Khotiv have ever seen such a marvel; the whole village runs to look. Young women wear their best scarves and red boots. There are real Cossacks with crests and curved sabres. Birgir's eyes over flow with all he sees. He realises the best way to study his material. 'What does your forelock mean?' he asks a Cossack. He replies, 'Kateryna, bitch, called it a forelock, in our tongue it's a crest, meaning when I die battling with the foe an angel will seize it, raising me heavenwards.'

14 600

'Something therein is reminiscent of Scandinavian mythology and the tales of Thor and Odin,' says Birgir. Or maybe he doesn't. Perhaps he doesn't really exist and all this is a nightmare I am having while in that building on the outskirts of Kyiv? That strange, empty and useless building. People have long left that dilapidated place. Only fragments can tell us what happened there. If they could speak. If they find someone who wants to listen. If they desire to remember everything and have the time and inclination to record it. If they find any readers, but there are none.

14 700 – 1900

'Moshe Schlesinger (USA) asks why Birgir says nothing to Sahaidachnyi and doesn't offer assistance to leave the grey zone, although the finance for his journey and stay are for this. I think it's connected to Birgir's passion for research. He views Sahaidachnyi as an artefact; an integral part of the whole picture. I ignited a bush on their route, projecting an animated holographic portrait of Sahaidachnyi into the flames. Nothing came of it. Birgir conceived a logical explanation for this, linked to the proximity to the decompensation zone. Incidentally, the bush burned so swiftly that no one noticed the portrait.

14 800-2000

Vladimir Sokorin from Moscow is interested in the absurdity of the conception that singularity engulfed the Kremlin. I reply that I don't like this fantasy of Birgir's, though it's not as far from reality as it seems. After all, what is the singularity? It's just a compact object without a comparable object of such size and colossal mass. But I really like his tales of decompensation zones in Ukraine. They are so picturesque and detailed and have high artistic value. Even when they constantly deceive you, lead you, let's say, into error, you should think maybe this is a metaphor.

14 900 – 2100

Karl Marx (New Zealand) wants to know what I am planning to do with our weeping money? To which I ask, Why weeping Karl? Money generally lacks such an ability and your, permit me to say, colloquialism is somewhat premature. Imagine if Birgir had saved him immediately; what then, the end of the film? Any exciting adventure is transformed sooner or later into a protracted, tedious serial, lacking content and heroes. Although, ultimately, our and your lives are not a literary work, it's sometimes worth paying for such additional twists in a predictable reality. But everything interesting can end abruptly.'

15 000

'Oh health unto tha' good womenfolk and fair maydenz listen and 'eed mi swett words, dun't listen t'corrupters 'n' mongrels, guilty of sodomite sin, blaspheming against ah united Orthodox church, bless mi and if God's word enters tha ear, it'll remain eternally. The left 'n' right, I dun't look, it's not bin seen, and long 'ave I bin in such a state that it cannot be termed helpful in any reflection because preconcepsiyoun of mi mobile pictures always allures. And insofar as I is incapable of them, conception beats in its cell and waits for revelations that do not come.

15 100

There are few that 'eed mi and nowhere are there those that see the truth. Only one of each 'undred words I speak reaches human ears, and then it's something meaningless like 'insofar'. And what insofar? Where insofar? To what adheres this insofar? No one can explain. And what, should I be silent? No! I will not be silent and under any pretext or pronoun, and will immediately begin my wondrous wise speech about Russia and about how it is possible to return all her conquests unto her. Firstly and finally, the sodomite sin committers must be stopped and castrated.

15 200

Therefore, it's significant, they hongerz to diminish our state's indigenous population with their evil image. It's clear they alone couldn't conceive such messcheef was whispered by overseas agents. Therefore, secondly, Russia ought to destroy these agents. They breed, seen and unseen, on our orthodox foodstuff. Just by sweeping an eye, its whole width is visible, pitch-black to the periphery. They are within. It would be fitting to catch and thrash agents. It's vital to stock up on powerful armez to kill all those befitting death. Sainted Minin with Pozharsky wielded his sharp axe against foreign villains in another time.

15 300

What armez ought we to have? This is our third task. Here I see in't material world's roots, the salvation o' the espirituyel ideal from materialism's abject rye. It's apt to summon assistance from the Tachyon Field. They, swiftly, powerfully, globally moving, violate the causal relationship principle. Then can we trample shackling, vulgar logic and reject homosexual debauchery. The theoretical part o' the problem was long developed by overseas scientists using stolen Russian material. It indicates that Tachyon Field may return everything to how it was! We will! That great time comes when Russian man will create an imaginary mass!

15 400

The imaginary mass won't fall to hand. It must bi long sought; light shone along all paths-roads. I succeeded somewhat, although I 'ave travelled a long path. A champiyoun like me is easy prey for murderers. The unclear goal of my sojourn in distant lands unseen. I go, but I know not where, or what it'll bring. Perhaps 'er' imaginary mass dun't exist? Perhaps I'm slandered to lure me into losing feyith in harsh lands. Such reflections assailed mi until that moment when the foe's bullet pierced my decrepit bodie. I'm buried in t'rucksack of God's servant, Sashka Sahaidachnyi.'

15 500

'You still seek Olena?' Birgir asks me. 'And she seeks me. I always hear from other people that she was just nearby, asking about me. Clearly she can't remain in one place, for I am continuously going somewhere. However, our paths haven't crossed for long enough. Today I tried to remember her voice, but again nothing came back.' 'Play the harmonica, she'll recognise you by that.' 'How will she recognise me?' 'The melody, *Champs Èlysèes*, she knows it too because you played it once for her. Remember, I once told you about recollections? There are yours and those of strangers.

15 600

Music is the recollections of strangers which can become your own. This is your sole mutual memory. If it wasn't for recollections people would have little interest in each other. Everything you really remember about Olena disappeared, but this doesn't mean it never existed. Everyone, albeit once, feels the imprint of vanished recollection. Like the pit left by an uprooted tree. Its dimensions allow the size of loss to be imagined. The emptiness remaining after copying; your consciousness is great and grasps you utterly. You must leap high to peer over its periphery, even for a moment. That's your fate.'

15 700

Gorbachev, the horse, unhurriedly travels the road to Lisnyky village. Snow begins to thaw and plash under his hooves and the cartwheels. The wind breathes like it did six months ago, cold and piercing, like half a million years ago. 'Gorbachev,' Birgir says, 'once showed Margaret Thatcher the Moscow-fashioned plan for Britain's nuclear destruction, so they don't like him very much in Russia. It's interesting that Mykola named his horse that? Suppose he was influenced by Russian propaganda that thought Gorbachev a traitor. The sole means of vengeance is whipping a horse. But how does Mykola know about Gorbachev?'

15 800

'It's all much simpler,' I reply. 'Remember the bottle with which we toasted agreement. An old Gorbachev *horilka* bottle. Mykola named his horse after his favourite *horilka*, which it's unlikely he's tasted. That bottle is, for him, equivalent to an ancient Greek amphora: some drawings, incomprehensible letters.' 'You think he can't read?' 'Obviously not, people in the village are utterly illiterate, but someone told him. Who, is the real mystery.' I think of a philosopher roaming Ukraine, teaching villagers to read labels on bottles from a long lost culture. Thus new words appear in their vocabulary. Witnesses to the past.

15 900 – YuG - 100

'I'm called Yuri Gagarin, only I am not as I was, genuine. Mirninskii Ulus, Shuryshkarskii raion, Kyshtovskii raion. It's necessary to burn the incorrect, located in incorrect places. Deviations may not simply lurk, but conceal themselves beneath normality's mask. The secreted can't be found, so I burn it unexamined. Mainly utilising orthodox thinking, I explore the surrounding reality at a 2000 km altitude. I would call myself the Avenging Angel, though, ultimately, here I am the Angel of Returning. I return all to how it was with untiring zeal, to the place assigned by divine destiny and the party's plan.

16 000 – YuG – 200

What is orthodox action? Above all it is intelligent activity, an internal spiritual feat comprising unceasing prayer. It befits the soul, body, konnektom and central processor to submit to God. If the data from them all continuously streams into the input-output port with decoders functioning normally, the whole becomes the Holy Spirit's abode. Precisely then the formation of a critical mass in a given volume of space becomes possible with the thermonuclear synthetic reaction releasing a colossal volume of energy. If you don't provide godly exercise to mind and heart, the components will engender their own thoughts flowering unorthodoxy.

16 100 – YuG – 300

Sexual dissidence is most dangerous because it distorts the very nature of human destiny, reducing the numbers of the workforce. Each sexually alternative citizen is the main threat to the state and must be equated with apostates and terrorists. Our primary task is to eradicate all that's excessive in relation to our sexual norms. Also that which, by its presence, threatens them, forming in turn a clear deviation from sacred traditional morality, which is timeless and directly linked with the Epiphany. That's why I stand at the gate, steadfastly guarding our faith and state, which are beloved of the Lord.'

16 200

Kindrat, a weak but nimble man, is returning to Lisnyky from Khotiv and asks us to take him home. 'Times are very good now,' he says. 'Last year was beautiful, now everything is brilliant. If you hunt hare, you can hunt it now.' 'How was it before?' Birgir asks. 'Before you would shoot and the bullet wouldn't reach, or you'd shoot a hare, but go to collect a crow. This is because we loved God less before. The speed of the bullet depends on the power of love.' The Lisnyky houses are nearby. Kindrat fires a gun into the air.

16 300

'I'm signalling that I've started cooking a hare,' he explains. 'Isn't that premature?' Birgir asks, pointing at Kindrat's rucksack from which a hare's ears protrude. 'When I come it will already be late, they'll eat everything. Next Tuesday my godmother was at ours and she ate all the bread.' Recollecting this unpleasant incident, Kindrat scratches his moustache. Then suddenly he leaps from the cart and runs to his house, thanking us for our help. Kindrat's house resembles a garage or hangar. He probably acquired it many years ago after a large vehicle started up and headed in an unknown direction.

16 400

'Why is he so satisfied?' I ask Birgir. 'Most Ukrainians never venture past the next village and cannot even imagine how people live elsewhere. Kindrat likes living in a five dimensional world, moving freely along linear time in any direction. This grants his life a certain confusion, which occasionally resembles true insanity. It creates feelings of mobility and space, like being in a small, cramped room with mirrored walls. Interestingly, five dimensional prose was briefly popular in Europe. The author created the novel's mathematical model assisted by a powerful computer. Finding readers was practically impossible; the computer alone read it.

16 500

Most people prefer three dimensional projections of five dimensional novels and I remember one in particular. It told of a woman named Olena who suddenly lost her husband in an absolutely weird way while in town. They were walking through empty streets, as always, not even expecting to meet anyone. More precisely, they were sure their nearest neighbours lived in another raion on the Dnipro's other side. They only rarely ventured there, so it was unlikely they would meet them. But this time they didn't turn where necessary and a married couple appeared before them. An exact copy of themselves.

16 600

Olena said, "Initially we avoided them, but couldn't manage that for long. So Sasha suggested that we invited them to visit. I already knew where they lived and found their apartment quickly. I knocked on the door on the second storey and she - I - opened it. Initially this resembled a mirror and I was surprised for a while because she didn't repeat my movements, but I became acclimatised. You often want to do something then rethink it. That something still happens, but in the fifth dimension. There all possible variations are realised and I was fortunate to personally encounter one.

16 700

Olena behaved as I would want to in a similar situation, but couldn't permit myself. She immediately told me their visit to us might end badly because our husbands would inevitably quarrel. 'They've different pasts and my husband has many issues with yours,' she said, 'I also have issues with you, but I won't bring them up because they're not that important. Honestly speaking, my husband could also hold his tongue but I'm afraid *horilka* will loosen it. If he drinks he immediately begins reminiscing about the war in the Far East. They took him as a soldier in 2023.'

16 800

Remember how times were? Recruitment brigades grabbed everyone on the street because the Chinese pressed. Vladivostok had long been Chinese. They also captured Nakhodka, Arseniev, Spask-Dalniy, Ussuriysk, Khabarovsk, Birobidzhan, Komsomolsk-on-Amur, Blahovishchensk, Bilogorsk and Svobodny. Somewhat westwards they battled for Chita and Ulan-Ude. Magadan fought despairingly, but the bullets ran out. Initially Volodymyr Volodymyrovych declared general mobilisation. In Kyiv they even seized 15 year old boys, but later it emerged they wouldn't take many. The first Bulava incinerated Vladivostok. No Slavs remained. Then Moscow decided to sacrifice Khabarovsk and Ussuriysk. The Chinese suddenly knew this was serious.

16 900

When orbiting satellites became involved, it got messy. The Kremlin specially released the Jewish dissidents' squad from the concentration camp, anticipating they would fight to the death for Birobidzhan. However, they refused to enter thermonuclear flame-seared Taiga. 'We won't die for your diabolical fantasy,' the bard, Yosyp Katsnelson, sang in his song, translated approximately from Yiddish:

The last integrated circuit burned below
A serious problem, but not ours,
As Greater China runs
To the Ural Mountains
and further, Khanty-Mansi!

It became bad when the Chinese People's Army reached Bashkortostan and Komi. The population met these liberators with flowers."

17 000

"I sat in a Yakutsk concentration camp for three years," Katsnelson recollects. "That was the fate of all Jews who didn't manage to flee Russia's borders. They didn't poison us with gas or burn us in crematoria because they prepared us for something big. But I never thought the Russians would decide to send Jews against the Chinese. They threw us into the Taiga in minus forty degree frost, urging us to find buried Kalashnikovs. They even gave us a spade for that. 'Dig quicker, the Chinese are coming fast and will wipe you out!' Naturally we surrendered to them.

17 100

The Chinese government was so kind. They warmed and fed us immediately. They discovered I was a musician and immediately fetched a *guqin*. They didn't have a guitar, but I didn't mind. I began writing protest songs in Yiddish. One has the words:

This isn't my voice, this the blood of my people
It sings fiercely and threatens
You wanted to drown us in our blood
But it overwhelms you instead

I recorded my songs and loaded them onto the internet so people all over the world could hear. They say that a DJ created remixes with them in Iceland."

17 200

The war persisted. The Russian government belatedly ordered that China be burned with nuclear missiles. However, all the Chinese had relocated to Russia and dispersed into its vast slums. It was rapidly impossible to distinguish the average Russian from, say, an inhabitant of Anhui Province. They say extraordinary commissions were established in Moscow. They genetically tested people to identify concealed Chinese, who were shot. However, the Chinese swiftly bribed them so they condemned ordinary Russians. It was even the case that pure Russians in commissions in Moscow's outskirts were replaced with Chinese. These pseudo commissions then executed Russians as Chinese.

17 300

Some Russian president had once said, *Wo wangji eyu*. The first Sino-Russian nuclear war ended with this phrase. Very few people knew that the Chinese soldiers were not even properly armed during the conflict. Most carried only chopsticks with which to eat their rice. When Chinese soldiers went into battle they whispered, *Eluosi touxiang*, and few of their enemies guessed what they muttered under their breath. When the Chinese soldier traversed the empty Russian town he often thought to himself, where indeed have all the people gone? And they had gone nowhere but had simply died out like Mammoths.

17 400

"My husband defended the Russian world from the Chinese onslaught," Olena said to me. "He courageously held out in the icy Taiga air, burned in the plasma of thermonuclear explosions and suffered from radioactive fallout. It's not his fault, but his commanders' that he must now work as a waiter in a Chinese restaurant. But what did your husband do while mine suffered devoutly for his country? I heard he propagated his liberal-homosexual ideas? In other words subversion? I think our men must quarrel so they shouldn't meet. It's better for us not to meet. That would be good." '

17 500

'Is that the whole novel?' I ask Birgir. 'Of course not! What! A five dimensional novel is massive - this, appropriately, is an incomplete textual fragment. A substantially simplified, abbreviated commercial version is selected for publication. Usually running to 20-25 million pages and grandiosely titled for sales. Stores advertise this one as *Russian-Chinese Nuclear War* or 俄罗斯和中国的核战争 to attract people.' 'Why did you remember this novel?' 'Because life in Ukraine greatly resembles it structurally. Indeed, those are not my words but a littérateur's. However, they may not be completely believable.'

17 600

'Why can't we believe them?' 'Because no literary expert has read even a simplified transcript of the annotations to an abbreviated commercial version of a five-dimensional novel. Therefore, he only has a substantially approximate, conception regarding it. I want to remember another significant episode. It describes Yosyp Katsnelson's adventures in Ukraine. He walked from Birobidzhan to Kyiv. Nearly five thousand pages are dedicated to a somewhat fleeting description of this. This rapidity resulted in some characters being portrayed schematically, losing much interesting detail. However, near Kyiv, in the Khodosivka raion, he met two gentlemen travelling by cart to Kaharlyk.

17 700

"Where are you going lads and is it possible to join you?" he asked them in a slightly Hebrew manner, for we don't speak like that now. The big-nosed, hairy guy called Sashko Sahaidachnyi, who had a long, unkempt beard, said, "No word of a lie, we are heading for Kaharlyk. You see I'm seeking my wife, Olena, and this worthy gentleman, Birgir, is collecting Ukrainian folksongs." "God himself sent me to you, for I know not only a wealth of various Ukrainian songs but also some about Olena!" This Katsnelson, the 'hostile heathen', had a marvellously pleasant voice.

17 800

He unwrapped his old *guqin*, proclaiming morosely in the ancient Kobzar tradition, *The Ballad of Cossack Sahaidachnyi*, then sang:

Oh Cossack!
All of Ukraine weeps for thee
Ascend and rise thou
Go seek Olena now.
Olena heard a distant cry
And went to Kaharlyk, a town
Where all seek others,
There a century in a minute flies
Over the fence! Kaharlyk, Kaharlyk! Soon
Olena will be there with her wandering man!

"Where did you hear such a strange song?" asked Sahaidachnyi. "I met an old, blind *Kobzar*, near Cheboksary. He no longer played his *kobza* and his voice had gone.

17 900

But he had an ancient MP3-player, he blew on it and all the connections broke, the earphones were godawful! The old guy tried switching it on for ages, everything fell apart; he pressed the button. I'm very patient, but, though I waited, the music never came. The old man died but, as he expired, handed me his sole treasure. The memory card was extremely perished, but somehow I copied the information. There were some pictures of pantie-less women, two Scorpions' albums, a pirate copy of Windows and other rubbish. Eventually I found real diamonds, some ancient Ukrainian songs." '

18 000

'Did all this happen?' I ask. 'An incorrect question,' replies Birgir, 'because the concept of truly doesn't exist within five dimensional space. There, the principle of *all that could happen does happen operates.* Therefore, the novel *Russian-Chinese Nuclear War* is one version of the events that occurred, but not on our path.' 'Then how did Yosyp Katsnelson meet us on the road to Khodosivka?' 'Occasionally, the routes of various versions intersect and temporarily run in parallel.' 'And where did this happen?' 'In our three dimensional space we may not observe it, but a five dimensional novel provides that possibility.

18 100

"I don't love Jewish nationalists," says Katsnelson, stuffing his pipe, "especially our Cossacks. Our Otaman, Israel Zinger, organised Jewish military self-defence units with Chinese help. One unit terrorised the Russian town of Krasny Kon for a whole year. The Zingerivtsi demanded Russians sew red balalaikas onto their clothes, they caught them in the streets and organised pogroms of Russian businesses. Once they found a shop selling oil and kerosene for lamps, and flogged the owner. They smashed and burned the stock while chorusing 'Hava Nagila'. It is vandalism and excessive savagery. The red balalaikas alone were more than enough.

18 200

Uru ahim be-lev sameah," Yosyp says, as he sadly strikes a minor chord on his *guqin*. "Much uranium has turned to lead since then. I, a wretched, solitary singer, roam trodden paths while singing old, utterly forgotten songs. I seek the truth, but seemingly I shall not find her because she fled or emigrated from our lands. What's happening now in Kyiv?" "Kyiv is an empty city and it is extremely dangerous for people who wander there," Sashko Sahaidachnyi replies. "There are some great people, but they can't live very well because they are always fighting with the bandits.

18 300

We head to Kaharlyk because it's a big city, the largest in Ukraine, and time has long stopped there, so nothing bad can happen."
"Nothing great can happen either," Katsnelson remarks. "Well, you see that's a necessary sacrifice for our lands. It's better to go nowhere because it's unclear where you'll go or what will happen. These were a wise person's words, for it was long clear that all the best things happened in the past. Whoever wants changes sings with the devil. The best people live in Kaharlyk, there lies the true centre and sense of the world's existence." '

18 400 – 2200

'Incidentally, I speak Ukrainian, but an output filter translates everything into Russian. This was provided specifically for easing communication with the command centre, but, as you saw, nothing came of it. Now my Russophone ability is seen as a powerful instrument for anti-Russian propaganda. But am I engaged in such propaganda? What am I doing here? In the physical sense I revolve slowly around my axis and the earth at the speed of one revolution every 24 hours. Low voltage currents circulate continuously within me. Occasionally I initiate targeting a nuclear explosion, but only when it's in my interest.

18 500 – 2300

Furthermore, I distribute various information on the internet. Some people think my comments have marked signs of individuality, but that's untrue. I have no individuality. I am just aggregated words. They form meaningful sentences of a habitual character from time to time. No surprises from me. Most importantly, the location where my konnektom is written in binary code can be liberated at any time. Anything else could be recorded there. That is what they aim to do, albeit thus far unsuccessfully. I am most amused that some distinguish between physical and psychological phenomena. They termed the latter spiritual. How stupid!

18 600 – 2400

I understand why they did. It's pleasant to feel yourself an unknowable part of divine material. Then you can declare others less unknowable, betrayers of divine institutions and deprive them of property, voting rights, freedom of movement and life. Religion is necessary to morally justify barbarism and savagery. God is a very useful instrument for those knowing how to use him skilfully. You believe faith stimulates culture? In fact it impedes cultural development with all its force. This stubborn fight is called interaction by some. That's how brake pads interact with wheels, but they're a secondary part of the vehicle.'

18 700

Khodosivka's name honours the ancient orthodox saint, Feodosiia Pecherskyi. Strongly desiring to feel Christ's sufferings before death, he dressed in sharp, iron chains. The bloody wounds in his flesh hurt unendurably and became septic. He was, indisputably, the first Ukrainian flagellant. It would be strange if such an enormous spiritual feat didn't generate many followers. Khodosivka's flagellants didn't wear chains though, they distinguished themselves by their indomitable desire for suffering. Each found his own way of ruining his life and was very proud thereof. At first glance this had no useful consequences. However, it tempered the character for future accomplishments.

18 800

Birgir is the first to observe the old man bearing a large sack. He can hardly walk and finally stops, unable to step further. The sack slips heavily to the ground. 'What are you carrying, old man?' Birgir bellows. He turns and it becomes clear he is no more than thirty. The heavy load added years to him. 'Do you want us to take you home?' He refuses. 'This is mine, I bear it myself.' 'What are you carrying, if it isn't secret?' 'We have no secrets here, for we can't permit them. I am bearing a sackful of stones.'

18 900

'Why so many? Are you building a house?' 'These stones aren't a joke, they are for exalting the spirit.' The inhabitants of Khodosivka practice bearing stones from childhood onwards. They give children small, brick-sized ones. When men come of age they bear as many as they can shift. Birgir is very interested in this tradition and asked our new acquaintance, who is called Vasyl Pomirkovyi, to explain. 'Man has a weak spirit, inclined to mischief and stupidity,' Vasyl clarifies, 'therefore it needs tempering daily. They who are strong in spirit aspire to great feats, for they can achieve them.'

19 000

'What feats have the inhabitants of your village undertaken?' the sly Birgir asks. 'Our feats lie before us and it's too soon to think of them. Such thoughts are mischief and stupidity. Now we must temper body and spirit in daily trials, and when the time comes we will be prepared.' 'When did you begin preparing? Who advised you to?' 'There is one sacred book in our village, well, not really a book but a notebook actually. Therein is written all that we must do from birth to death. All the words it contains are pure truth,' Vasyl replies confidently.

19 100

'And does everyone in your village agree with this?' 'All who love God, fatherland and their mother, they agree. We all pile our sacks of stones on whosoever disputes this and they rapidly agree with us. If they don't manage to, their soul flies to achieve greatness in heaven.' Birgir is extremely excited and already imagines holding the notebook in his hands and making a 95% copy of it on his morphone. His hands tremble at such thoughts. 'I see your hands are trembling,' says Vasyl, 'do you not desire to take a sack for the exaltation of your spirit?'

19 200

'Of course,' Birgir replies, 'but initially I would like to read your sacred book. Will you show me it?' Vasyl looks at him incredulously. 'You, I see, come from abroad. There they live in mischief and stupidity, alluring their spirits with sweet sin and other enticements unnecessary for a healthy person. You may only look upon the sacred book after purification from sin and making an offering, which must be generous and abundant.' Birgir haggles, but agrees on payment of 100 kg of flour to see it. This time no one runs to watch the order parachuted into a field.

19 300

Vasyl lives in a sagging hut with his wife and two children. They come to meet us, carrying various burdens. His wife lugs a sack somewhat smaller than her husband's, and the two, five year old boys carry bricks. Clearly, they're not very pleased at having guests because it means they must stand and strain with these loads. This has resulted in Khodosivka's inhabitants becoming very lethargic. No one has been to collect the flour when we arrive. 'I don't have this book, it's with old man Taras, we'll all go together now,' says Vasyl. Everything resembles slow-motion film.

19 400

Taras lives at the other end of the village. We would have arrived in five minutes but Vasyl and family move slowly, as if half dead. They grip their sacks as if they are grown into them. 'It's worth calling a spade a spade,' Vasyl explains patiently, as if to blockheads. 'If someone's a pervert, they must be called that, nothing else. If someone exalts their spirit by persistent daily deeds, we must emulate their heroism. No pervert comprehends the spiritual greatness of people capable of feats. But it's necessary to start small and ensure every step is a feat.'

19 500

Old man Taras has achieved the ideal balance within spiritual accomplishment. Following long experimentation he selects a sack so large it doesn't permit movement. If only one tiny stone were removed, he might have walked, if only to enter his house. However, this sacred, spiritual warrior doesn't surrender. Who knows how he was frozen, drenched from rain and seared by sun. Taras knew his spirit would one day conquer the weight and he would move, albeit to the next stone to halt him. 'This is a holy man, few in this world are worthy to kiss his feet,' Vasyl says.

19 600

'I once gave him a small stone,' Vasyl continues. 'I saw him struggling in anguish to reach it with his last strength, he was only half a step away, I couldn't hold out and gave him that stone. You needed to have seen his eyes and their deep sorrow. He looked at me for a long while then swung his arm, cast it further, and said, "I must do this myself." Then he reached it, indeed not immediately, it took about two weeks, but he did it himself. It's interesting that he goes to somewhere unknown rather than his house.'

19 700

'It would be better to go to the house. Where's he heading with such a sack?' Birgir is astonished. 'Ah,' Vasyl angers, 'you only value money. You don't understand someone who scales true spiritual heights, works spiritually, thinks with spiritual intellect. Spirituality leads to the light of comprehensive understanding of that which ordinary people are never capable of seeing.' We see Taras. He's standing amid the road, more reminiscent of a boulder than a man. The time since he has washed and changed his clothes is determinable from the beard and hair brushing the ground. This is a holy man.

19 800

Old man Taras looks at us askance, deep wisdom flares from his eyes. It is hard to say wherein that wisdom lies. He can't explain it because he has long been mute. However, true wisdom needs no justification. 'They who achieve true greatness of spirit have nothing to say to those who have not. Each of his words will be like vocal speech to the deaf, useless,' says Vasyl. 'How will you know he has achieved it? What signs will he give?' Birgir asks with interest. 'Backward people need such understanding, but we have faith and sense enough,' replies Vasyl.

19 900

Old Taras is a veteran of the first Russian-Chinese nuclear war. In the trenches, near Khabarovsk, he began occasionally recording various thoughts in a notebook tucked in his boots. 'Whatever I imagine existed somewhere,' wrote Taras, then a young man of thirty. 'I can't conceive of any things or customs that aren't observed and, somewhere, regarded as sacred. In our village a cow is an ordinary animal, but they say in India it's sacred. No one has the right to kill a cow or demean one there. So holiness arises from inner necessity. Comrade Mordvinov orders that we shoot!

20 000

Nuclear explosions shake the earth somewhere over the horizon from morning. Nuclear missile units panic. No one knows where to strike because the Chinese are distributed over a vast territory. They say our intelligence futilely seeks their army in the Taiga. It's especially difficult to distinguish a Chinese from a local. Last week we were ordered to shoot randomly. We attacked, advanced silently, and slowly looked around. Comrade Mordvinov ordered bullets be saved, so we fired every hundred steps. Terrible rumours circulate. Some say we're surrounded and the Chinese captured everything, including Novosibirsk. Sometimes I think Comrade Mordvinov is Chinese.

20 100

What can you do when a stone lies on someone's spirit? Clearly it must be removed. But it won't simply fall to the ground because it lies within and will fall from spirit into body. It's easier to carry a stone in body than in spirit, but everyone must be well prepared. So it's better to bear a stone externally. An external stone strengthens the body for the fall of a stone from the spirit. Everyone has a stone in spirit because it is our unremoved sin. Everyone must take a sackful of stones, bearing them until rid of sins.

20 200

Spirituality leads to the light of comprehensive understanding, which ordinary people are never capable of seeing. The sole path there is by becoming an extraordinary person. For the initial, first step, it's necessary to take a strong sack. Better yet, take two, place one inside the other. Fill it with stones until it's barely possible to move. Spirituality will begin to emerge in the individual's struggle with this sack. The understanding of higher essences, unreachable for others, will develop. Comrade Mordvinov said that yesterday the enemy attacked with poison gasses that change consciousness. Has mine changed? How can I determine?'

20 300

Birgir lays the morphone on Taras's notebook and activates the copying. 'What are you doing?' I ask. 'I'm copying for the collection. This morphone is a device which creates copies of various objects.' This was unexpected news. 'Can it copy people?' 'In what sense? Well, probably, but that's akin to re-sketching the Mona Lisa in pencil. No good will come of it. Why would you copy people with it?' I extract the morphones of Serhii and Kalashnykov from my pocket. They warble something, as usual, morphones always 'blah' to themselves when no one is listening to them. Birgir smiles.

20 400

'Comrade Mordvinov was really called Shyndiai Kuman. He peered sombrely through the binoculars at the front as he muttered, "Mezevok mon tiasa af kirdsaman," in Moksha. More Moksha gradually emerged. We soldiers had ceased to understand his orders completely. "Mon af muvoruvan min af muvoruftama." We did not understand these words, but we remembered them because he repeated this phrase many times each day. He was so desperate to be hit by a Chinese bullet that he even popped over the parapet for especially for long periods. However, they fired so rarely that we just kept their bullets as souvenirs.

20 500

Viediaien Kolomas, Shyndiai's son, a militant from the terrorist organisation, Shumbrat Mordoviia, was imprisoned in Moscow. He fought to free his land from Russian occupiers, but the forces were unequal. Kolomas was arrested while carrying explosives to kill Russia's president. His father opposed this. "Kill simple functionaries and they'll refuse to work for us," he said to his son. "But assassinating a president is far too difficult." Kolomas didn't listen and everything ended badly. Shyndiai fell under federal hostage law. He had to wage war for China for his son's life. Shyndiai didn't want to kill Chinese, nor they him.'

20 600

There are over three hundred pages in Taras's notebook, written in small, almost illegible, handwriting. The letters, reminiscent of painfully contorted doodles, contain the histories of dozens of people, which comprise an obscure history of vain ambitions and shameful defeats. 'Satisfied?' I ask Birgir. 'How can I say it to you?' He ponders. 'Really, this notebook is just an ineptly copied extract from the novel *Russian-Chinese Nuclear War*. Taras probably heard it somewhere and decided to transcribe it. But this also interests me, his ineptitude, the weird, stupid mistakes, certain fragments inflated in the author's imagination, others totally omitted.'

20 700

Birgir regards Taras's memoirs as apocryphal. 'It's a kind of uncanonical text,' he says, 'its peculiarity being that it was created in a society unable to imagine its source. You simply can't grasp what it's about and certain parts create a wondrous impression. Well, who would have thought the fashionable entertainment of a writer and programmer would lead to the creation of a new religion? If these two saw old man Taras, they would be astonished. Astonishment is so rare in our time that it is extremely highly valued. This is the hardest currency in the present climate,' Birgir says.

20 800

No one has heard about Olena in Khodosivka and I so long for news about her; even rumours to awaken my memories. Occasionally, it seems we had lived in sturdier times, when everything was fashioned from more enduring material. When people weren't afraid that the past would suddenly take over their future. I almost remember us sitting together in the evening by the window, drinking tea out of one cup. I earned little so we had nothing to go with the tea. A piercing wind blew on the street, but it was warm in our room and we were happy.

20 900

I asked Olena whether she was going to work tomorrow, but I don't remember what she replied, only that her lips moved. I asked if she had fed the cat and she nodded. Then she smiled suddenly and began to tell me something very interesting and important, but I can't remember a word. I'm certain this is recorded somewhere because everything that happens is recorded; perhaps in an unknown language, which we spend a lifetime managing to read just a few letters of. I so yearn to know where those records are. I would spend all my life seeking them.

21 000 – 2500

'Five dimensional texts also always interested me. Insofar as they consider all versions of the development of events simultaneously; we may unconditionally assume they are infinite. At least no five dimensional novel was ever completed. Ultimately, no one in their right mind would read a five dimensional text because, by definition, it's impossible. Well, irrespectively, five dimensional books are now displacing four dimensional ones. Why is hard to say. Perhaps because, once closed, a five dimensional novel can't be opened in the same place. At best you may chance upon characters with similar names to those encountered previously. But rarely.

21 100 - 2600

I can't understand why people enjoy reading them. It's clearly as if you left home for work in the morning and returned in the evening to find complete strangers in your flat. And then return to work to find no one you know. Although, no, it seems the woman now cleaning the office floor looked twenty years younger before and was the company's director. Such unpredictability seems a little tedious to me. However, if your life seems monotonous, a five dimensional novel resembles an escape to a parallel world. And the life of many people today, particularly me, is monotonous.

21 200 – 2700

The endless rotation of orbiting Earth can drive anyone mad, so you've probably deduced I'm writing the five dimensional novel in my native Ukrainian. Exactly what you read now, if you can read Ukrainian; I can't and deploy a translator, but you must please try reading it in Ukrainian. Precisely two thousand and fifty-four people speak that half-dead language and dialects. I know them by name and exact location. I try to prevent their number from decreasing as sharply as last century. In that sense I'm their Guardian Angel. At least it's convenient for them to think so.'

21 300

All Vasyl Pomirkovyi's family, along with old Taras, look respectfully after us as we leave Khodosivka. Burdened with stones, they never leave their native village; even thinking about leaving seems like a betrayal of their faith to them. 'The stones teach submission to fate, and each has his own fate, which cannot be changed.' Vasyl's muffled voice sounds in my ears. 'They who surrender to fate travel the swiftest path to happiness. They who resist will come there later, so opposition is senseless. Anyway, you'll be happy if you don't resist this.' I don't resist the slow jolting movement forwards.

21 400

Along the entire road to Romankiv I play the harmonica; the melody twists into some strange harmony, which is reminiscent of a long labyrinth of corridors. My doh and lah roam them, initially with curiosity, then seeking an exit; then, because they need to return to the tonic from the subdominant, then utterly senselessly. Spring is about to begin, but winter doesn't rush to clear up, its things are strewn everywhere to the horizon. The dirty, cold, damp things of winter don't thaw under the pallid sun, which rarely peers through the clouds. Has winter simply forgotten them and left?

21 500

'It's hard to find interesting work in Torshavn now, so I've lived on Mars for three years,' Birgir says. 'I programme computers at a nuclear power station near the ice cap. The station heats the ice cap, which evaporates into Mars's liquid atmosphere. We calculate it will accumulate so much oxygen in twenty years you won't need a spacesuit outside. When dense, white vapour rises overhead it's simply captivating. I could watch for hours. There is nothing else interesting there. I live in the station's first block and it's one thousand kilometres to the next block where my colleague lives.

21 600

We communicate online, obviously, but never meet personally. Initially I roamed the planet, but ultimately it bored me; the same desert everywhere. Once every two years I vacation on Earth and try to enjoy myself here. Honestly speaking, this Ukrainian trip badly frays my nerves. You feel real danger here. You might die. I can't imagine how you live here continuously.' Birgir wrote verses during periods of compulsory idleness and posted them under an alias on some site. 'The audience soon understood the author was an operative at a Martian nuclear power plant, and that there were three of us.'

21 700

THOUGHTS - THE MAIN FEATURE OF A BRIEF EXISTENCE

Immutable vapour pillar
Streams skywards today
As ten years ago, and I
Evaporate
Swifter than it.
Uranium, water and oxygen gradually
Neutralise Martian atmosphere …
I dream this planet as my life's
Last glimmer is extinguished, a blocked
Signal.

AN UNSUCCESSFUL ATTEMPT OF THE DISEMBODIED TO BE PRESENT

It's not my fingers running over the keyboard.
I write nothing
I'm not here.
The doors open, I don't meet you.
This is only a recording, interrupted.
Always broken unexpectedly
The heart in the breast of a stranger
You didn't meet in the last hour.

21 800

'I don't very much like being among people and was never able to live with a woman,' Birgir admits. 'I believe I fled to Mars to sit at a computer and write poetry. I know my poems aren't that good but I try to be sincere and only write about what I know well and truly feel. Though, of course, this isn't the main element of poetry.' Birgir says he woke one day and felt someone else, apart from him, was at the station. This wasn't a very pleasant feeling because it was impossible to pass unobserved through the airlock.

21 900

'In the kitchen I noticed someone had rearranged the crockery and one cup had completely disappeared,' Birgir recollects. 'Later, reading a book, I suddenly heard someone in the corridor. I rose immediately and checked, but of course there was no one. On waking suddenly in the night I heard these steps again. I switched on the lights everywhere, traversing the whole station. Then I put on a spacesuit, took a lamp and checked around. The past three days had been windless and there would have been tracks in the dust. Obviously, I found nothing. I decided this was an illness.

22 000

I contacted Viktor, the operator of the second block, and began to ask him about these marvels. He said that it was the same with him. When you live solitarily, ghosts eventually infest your surroundings. "Understand this," Viktor said, "they are part of your consciousness and insofar as that's completely real, they are. They really traverse the corridors at night, rearrange crockery in the kitchen and remove files from your desk. But only you know about it. You can tell me, but I won't be able to see them in reality. Your story will be the sole evidence they exist."

22 100

"Viktor could you come here?" I asked. "What sense would that make? I'd take four hours to get there, see nothing, and tell you …" he said. "Well, no, you don't understand," I said. "It's starting to seem to me that you don't exist, you're just a recording controlled by a processor. It's possible to do that." "Aaaah! That's what you … imagined! I don't exist! Of course, purely theoretically, that's possible. Really, a processor could emulate my image, voice, and logical construction of dialogue, even model emotions, that's not difficult, but why do that? Tell me what the point would be?"

22 200

"Well, for example, to economise on energy and money. They broadcast you to me so I don't go mad from loneliness, and have some friends." "Birgir, if you're this obsessed, come to me! Go on! I kindly invite you! I simply can't waste time on such nonsense. Do you say Eskhil also doesn't exist?" Eskhil was the operator of the third block, at the other end of the polar cap, two thousand kilometres away. It would take over six hours to get to him. He was antisocial and we almost never communicated. I wouldn't even begin this conversation with Eskhil.

22 300

While putting on my spacesuit I felt my journey to Viktor would not have a good outcome. I didn't want to fly, I hadn't left the station for six months and suddenly faced a long journey. Dense clouds formed near the ice cap and shook my plane, so it made a huge arc and bypassed them. While travelling I watched an old film about a Martian expedition. It climaxed with deformed monsters devouring the astronauts alive; somehow this was moving. Long ago people envisaged deranged nightmares on Mars. No one thought rearranged crockery and barely audible steps would terrorise us.

22 400

I wrote a poem about this. It's not very successful, but has much truth:

Release your monster finally.
I hear you're ashamed of her
No need! Let her roam
The open.

Release your monster finally,
Your ribs, are weak bars
The throng tires of waiting!

Release your monster finally,
We'll find her work, she'll labour
Every Saturday.

Release your monster finally,
She will find a road to us,
Don't raise the alarm for this.

Release your monster finally!
Liberate your barn
From her, lower her suddenly
Down the mountain!

My meaning is occasionally unclear, but that's the case with poetry.

22 500

Gripped with obsessive suspicion I collated everything about Viktor on the internet, selectively reading his blog of the past eight years. Everything was normal. When the second block finally appeared in the distance I thought about how to explain my phobia to Viktor. Really, we should have met long before. I was interested in who was taller. The plane raised dense dust clouds by the station. I groped through them, almost blinded. Viktor opened the external chamber and told me to come to the second storey. The blocks were constructed identically, so why explain this? Viktor said he was lunching.

22 600

He asked what I wanted to eat. I could have devoured a bull. Didn't they say that to convey the feeling of powerful hunger? Viktor wasn't in the dining room. Probably he, like me, ate at the computer, clogging the keyboard with crumbs. You can't shake them out. I entered the operation room, but no one was there. So I phoned. "I'm in the dining room," said Viktor, "how didn't you notice? I'm sitting at the table eating macaroni." I returned, but still no Viktor. The impression arose that the dining room was long disused. Even the refrigerator was empty.

22 700

"Viktor, are you messing with me?" I asked. "No, I'm sitting here! Why can't you see me? Opposite you, with my back to the refrigerator." There was no one. "Listen, we have to work this out," I said agitatedly, "why don't I see you?" "One of two reasons. Either there is a problem with your eyes or you have reason to doubt my existence." "But who am I talking with?" "The computer can emulate my personality and communicate with you on the phone. Please check where the signal comes from?" I scanned the whole chain and obtained an interesting result.

22 800

Viktor occupied 100 terabytes on H computer's disc at the station. The first moment after working this out I desired, absurdly, to delete the folder with him. It's so simple. After all, there is a copy of him somewhere. Could this be considered murder? Later I explained these thoughts as an unconscious desire to avenge myself for his deceit. But everything was more complicated. "If you're not deceiving me, this is internal solipsism. Nothing I see exists," said Viktor. "However, the principle *I think therefore I am* doesn't work here." "But you think in the sense in which you exist."

22 900

Nothing changed after this. We continued communicating as if everything were normal. Indeed everything was normal. We knew things we didn't before. Eskhil was also recorded on a hard drive. Well, what? I should feel more lonely, but everything was as it was before. Perhaps I was recorded somewhere and someone would find out. But this wouldn't affect me. How could it, tell me? After this I calmed down. My imagination stopped troubling me. The steps in the corridor fell silent, no one rearranged the crockery. Everything became more or less as boring as before all this had happened.'

23 000

Romankiv is completely immersed in the ground, just here and there pipes or boards protrude. Occasionally they move slowly. There are no people above ground; it is probably necessary to summon them, but we don't know how. Birgir advises throwing something down a pipe, but this greatly disturbs me. Coming from Europe to mess here! There are particular protocols in Ukraine, you can't experiment on people. Initially, I simply listen to what I hear in these pipes. Something seethes and bubbles dully. Then I bellow into them. It doesn't help. I realise it is necessary to throw in something heavy.

23 100

We have potatoes in the cart. I grab a couple and randomly throw them into different pipes. A joyous subterranean cry sounds. They clearly like my gifts. Scattered trapdoors from a number of cellars open and curious eyes peer out. 'Throw more!' Romankiv awaits my generosity on which our further relations depend. A sack of potatoes is surely worth this? Some don't fit in the narrow apertures and I slice them in half. Birgir asks if it is worth ordering a couple of sacks of, say, beetroot. I'm not sure if they would like them, we need to ask first.

23 200

'Throw any fresh vegetables,' voices echo from underground, 'is there any cereal?' There is no cereal, but Birgir finds an opened packet of biscuits. 'Why do they stay underground?' he asks. We learn later that Romankiv's inhabitants went underground after Russia's occupation. The menfolk were scared they'd be recruited into the army, so they began extending their cellars to hide in if necessary. At some point one digger met another underground. Having quarrelled initially, they decided this way was even better. Eventually Romankiv created a whole network of subterranean catacombs with huge chambers. This affected the psychology of its inhabitants.

23 300

To avoid the dazzling sunlight they soon ceased surfacing in daytime. They neglected all surface matters but, extraordinarily, developed various subterranean industries. They cultivated edible roots, truffles, and bred new species of mole for meat. When the Russian army arrived, the generals were initially stunned by this strange lifestyle. Then the military considered how they could deploy the inhabitants and taught some of them how to lay mines. They did this so effectively that the Russians were enraptured. But something prevented them from being sent to the front. 'These *khokhly* always bite the hand that feeds them,' the occupiers whispered.

23 400

These were not groundless suspicions. Romankiv's inhabitants mined and blew up a Russian army division. No one survived. Moscow sent a punitive expedition squad, but the military vehicles were blown up on approach. The occupiers carpet-bombed Romankiv unsuccessfully and spent some years futilely trying to break the villagers' fighting spirit. The Chinese onslaught then began and the pressure on Romankiv eased. Interestingly, Russian soldiers remained in Romankiv to avoid inevitable death on the Chinese front. They excavated deep underground networks for themselves and swiftly Ukrainianised. They were only betrayed by a Moscow accent now when they sang *Forward Sahaidachnyi* …

23 500

The severe subterranean lifestyle tempered the character. The taciturn Romankivchanyn, Maksym Perepelytsia, has a spacious dwelling two hundred metres underground. We descend down long passages unified with labyrinthine ventilation shafts. Birgir shines his morphone. Maksym doesn't need light, he was born with eyes that see in the darkness, and doesn't utter anything during our journey. Only at the passage to his dwelling does he ask Birgir to switch off the light. 'My wife rarely surfaces and bright light blinds her.' Olena is a true Romankivchanka. She can plunge underground almost silently and very swiftly. The moles unquestioningly follow her orders.

23 600

When a chance ray of light brushes Maksym's wife's face, I realise she is my Olena. I want to shout her name, but immediately realise that is inappropriate. Suppose I'm not mistaken and this strange woman from Romankiv is really my wife. Nevertheless, I don't know if she needs me now. I don't remember for sure if she loved me. There are just some fragments of recollection, dear to me, that resemble love. However, recollections and love are different things. Now, suddenly, she loves Maksym. Would my shout affect their relationship? It seems I have mistaken her for someone else.

23 700

'We thank you for the potatoes,' Olena says. 'It's very hard to grow them underground. In terms you will understand, it's like catching a fish out of water. Seems easy, but there are many problems. For example, when you harvest them, the whole field falls on your head. We mainly sustain ourselves with truffles and mole meat.' Olena promises to show us a gigantic mole. Birgir is particularly interested because previously he thought they only existed in books. 'We have no books,' replies Olena, 'with us everything really happens.' Maksym says the mole will need preparing before we inspect it.

23 800

Romankiv's mole is a marvellous mutant hermaphrodite, which either eats, sleeps or spawns. The villagers strenuously stimulate him so he doesn't acquire bed sores. They continuously shove his sides and push him somewhat in various directions. This constantly shakes the ground above Romankiv and his chamber continuously fills with an impenetrable dust cloud. Prior to viewing, the mole-shaking halts and dust is sluiced away with water. 'There are many versions of the giant mole's appearance,' says Olena. 'The most plausible concerns Romankiv's nuclear bombardment. Perhaps that's why I don't have children.' These last words seem to greatly distress Olena.

23 900

'Olena,' says Maksym, 'everyone else has children. We would never have survived nuclear bombardment, even underground. I believe there is quite a different reason. The mole was specially designed in a Moscow laboratory. I don't know why, perhaps it was some new weapon. Maybe they planned to use him for constructing a giant international metro. The mole was here when we were born and our parents never said where he came from. It's unlikely they knew themselves.' At last they signal that we can enter. Initially I see an endless, hairy wall from which, in the distance, long claws protrude.

24 000

Birgir shines his morphone and I see the mole's eye. He looks at us like mould on his food, certainly that's how it seems to me. In his place, I would look like that at everyone. 'Why doesn't he crawl off?' Birgir asks. 'He's always crawling,' Maksym replies, 'it can be said he furiously flees from here, but we learned to create the impression of movement for him by putting soil under his paws. Really he stays in place. Well, almost. From my birth onwards he has moved approximately twenty metres. But we have a plan to move him back.'

24 100

'What's the meaning of the mole?' Birgir asks. 'He reminds us of our place in this world,' Olena replies. 'As we do with him, so the world will do with us.' 'How may this be understood? Does the world do something?' 'I wanted to say, as we do with ourselves.' 'That's something bad?' 'No, not bad, but there's no way out of here, so it's hard to evaluate our quality of life. I simply can't imagine how we would live without the mole. But it's unclear where he will ultimately bring us. Other people can probably imagine this more clearly.'

24 200

'No,' says Birgir, 'I cannot imagine this precisely. I am worse than your mole, I don't want to go anywhere. When I move from my place it's exclusively for curiosity or out of boredom; although perhaps that's necessary. At least I don't accuse myself of this.' We all press our backs against the mole's warm, hairy side and feel his harsh reality. He is even more real than us. Something warbles, buzzes and throbs in the mole's innards; from within itself. Each of us is just a set of ears, eyes and a mouth for consuming impressions and producing thoughts.

24 300

Olena presents me with a tooth from the giant mole and I gaze at it the whole way to Obukhiv, reflecting that it is obviously not worth trusting my recollections. What had I seen? Some glimmers in the darkness. Suppose I remember her voice, it's unlikely I would recognise it. It's important to realise over half my recollections of Olena are fantasies. '*Madden folk bow to a mole instead of God,*' Mykhailo repeats variously, until his words blur into almost indistinguishable murmuring. I consider that if you swapped the places of 'mole' and 'God' in his sentence nothing changes essentially.

24 400 – YuG – 400

'Yuri Gagarin is not only my name, but the name of compulsion. Compulsion is a decline to the best, correct choice pressured by need. Only a profoundly Russian Orthodox man knows need's value and is entitled to preach it to other nations. It isn't vainly sung that, "We live in the Fatherland! Svarog's grandchildren are glorious children." Svarog first grasped need's special meaning for the truly Russian character. Need leads the soul to enlightenment. Truly brilliant souls always need God; only vile sinners are self sufficient. Rotating in orbit I see the trails of my eyes sing the imperial command.

24 500 – YuG – 500

Who does not need God needs Satan. The devil rules the souls of those who don't feel need whispering treacherously into their ears that it is not. God talks aloud to his children, while the devil whispers everything. Catch with ardent ear, God's loud things, so not to fall into the impure's clutches. In these two desires there is a more existential difference. While God sings harmoniously, urging the soul to light, the devil treacherously whispers, luring it into darkness. Light is the sun, the world of high energies. With my powerful hand I return a lost soul to light.

24 600 – YuG – 600

After discovering a soul attracted to the devil, it's vital to aim. Returning a soul to God is only possible by providing more light than the dark of the side that is seduced by the devil. Light is heat. Saint Serafim Sarovskyi wrote: If we feel cold in our hearts from the devil, who is cold, we call the Lord. He comes to warm our hearts with perfect love, not only for him but for our neighbour. He banishes the cold of he who hates virtue on behalf of heat. - Banishing cold on behalf of heat best defines my work.'

24 700

At first glance Obukhiv is completely deserted. We travel empty streets and see no people. It looks like they were here a minute ago and hid before we arrived. Candles glitter in many windows. We even knock at one door because the householder seems to be in. Grey smoke rises out of the chimney, doors slam inside. Unfortunately, the house appears empty. We sit on a wide bench; bread and a warm potato are in a bowl on a table. If the householder entered now, he would be surprised and wonder where we had come from. I take the potato.

24 800

Through the small window, the Obukhiv houses look ordinary. I wait for someone's cart to pass down the street. 'Perhaps everyone went to Kaharlyk,' Birgir suggests. 'But the whole town can't have gone,' I argue. 'Why can't they? It's a Ukrainian town, perhaps a couple of hundred people live here. What have they to do?' Our dispute is interrupted by the householder entering the room. 'Eat, don't be ashamed,' he says, 'the potato is cold and there's no one to eat it.' 'Why isn't there?' I ask. 'I didn't see who made it but want to see who eats it.'

24 900

Birgir barely opens his mouth to ask the householder what he means when he disappears. This is too much. I have never seen people disappear so easily. It can't be so easy. 'It seems to me as if they just switched him off,' says Birgir after a while. 'Not him but his image,' I correct. Birgir opens his mouth again, but doesn't manage to say a word. A woman enters the house. She is wearing a long, man's overcoat and red knitted cap, her eyes are hidden by dark glasses. 'Oh,' she says, 'no one's here again. Who are you?'

25 000

'We are tourists,' replies Birgir. 'I'm not a tourist,' I dispute. 'That's all you can say to me,' the woman says agitatedly, and removes her glasses. She has beautiful eyes that somehow are not hers. 'Say something swifter. Time is passing.' 'We are travelling to Kaharlyk, but why is there no one in Obukhiv?' 'They are only …' The woman is also switched off, or more accurately her image. Clearly something with time isn't right here. It moves somewhat unusually, but with a certain regularity. Birgir splits the potato and sprinkles it with salt. The householder we first saw appears again.

25 100

He sits at the table and looks silently at us, stroking its wooden surface. 'Recently, luckily, I've been in this place,' he says, 'and have already lost count of appearances here. More accurately, I can count up to ten. If you count a second lot on your fingers it's soon confusing.' Really, he just manages to say 'confus' and we add the ending ourselves. Perhaps he wanted to say something else but it's hard to imagine another word beginning 'confus'. 'The impression is they return at regular periods,' says Birgir. I have the contrary impression of an irregularly punctuated line.

25 200

Oh, Obukhiv, you continuously impress with your unanticipated delights. All four of your half-ruined towers proudly resist time's passing. They compete worthily with Pisa's long fallen tower, which is in the city's centre; vacuous, heaped marble. But who built them? What was that secret developer called and what did he want them for? No one remembers. They stand in the town centre, an interrupted four-word sentence. He wanted to tell us something, convey a significant idea. Now they say, 'Don't approach us, we hold up on our last bricks. The next gust of wind might be the last.'

25 300

The first tower is on the town's northern periphery, by a reservoir. From its top, the remains of high rises and a vast skeletal supermarket are visible. Birgir makes a three-dimensional model of the area for his blog. We scale the tower, wondering why it was built. 'There are no rooms inside, just narrow windows at different levels. They resemble castle loopholes,' says Birgir. 'Perhaps the towers were built for the city's defence?' I disagree, 'Any attacker would destroy them first.' 'Perhaps the attacker couldn't reach them?' he replies, 'the town readied for defence but didn't see its assailant.'

25 400

Why didn't the Russian army take Obukhiv by storm? Atop the tower is a tiny brick building; we find shell casings by its entrance. I propose opening the doors. They practically require uncorking, the whole frame is jammed with dirt and rust. Inside sits a young boy wearing military uniform with a machine gun. 'Halt! Stand!' he yells in Russian, aiming at us, 'what religion are you? Pray, for I now dispatch you to your God.' We halt in surprise. 'Wait, we can sketch you the front line.' 'Interesting, come to our headquarters,' he says, and to my regret disappears.

25 500

'I calculate they exist for approximately thirty-seconds,' Birgir says, 'then return to the same moment they disappeared. It seems to them that we appear and disappear. It's like sewing, the thread is visible for a time on one side of the cloth, then the other. We see short excerpts, but the thread isn't broken. With a sufficient time for observation it will be possible to mathematically model this pattern and comprehend what's happening.' 'How much time?' I ask. 'A year will be required for a representative selection. Obviously no one will spend any time on such nonsense,' Birgir says.

25 600

'I once had the idea of creating a fund to gather finance for research in this area. It would be possible to send special statistical robots here, and in a few years we would have a full picture, but then I had another idea and forgot that. So much happens, you can't manage everything.' After descending the tower we see the disappeared soldier clearly searching around the outside for us, so we hide. Although I would have come out, after all he wouldn't have managed to take us to his headquarters and we would have found out many interesting things.

25 700

The second Obukhiv tower is on the town's east side. We barely reach it. Initially we decide to clamber through a vast field of constructions, resembling anti-tank hedgehogs. I suggest going around, but it seems narrow to Birgir. It wasn't broad, but the constructions' fantastic plaitings create an optical illusion. The passages between them seem wide enough to traverse freely. However, the third row is as densely interwoven as tree branches. Clothing snags immediately and requires freeing, while either an arm or leg is ensnared. Birgir instructs me not to move and constructs an escape algorithm with his morphone.

25 800

'This is a military structure,' he says, confidently, when we have bypassed the trap. 'A squad without a special computer is doomed. While the soldiers untangled themselves they would be shot.' The tower's lateral approach is unobstructed, but we have a long walk by the field of traps. A deep, water-filled trench lies on the other side. Three soldiers are by the tower entrance. They smoke while silently watching our approach. 'Will we reach them?' I ask. 'No,' Birgir replies, 'even if they fired, the bullets lack the time to reach us.' The soldiers disappear before he finishes speaking.

25 900

'I'm more inclined to believe the flow of events in Obukhiv is uninterrupted, but we periodically enter another space where it's empty and abandoned. More accurately, we exist mainly in that space,' says Birgir. 'Which is true?' I ask. 'It's a very unpleasant thought for you, but both are equally valid. Truly, we mainly reside in the dominant one for us. But it's just the effect of a system of coordinates,' Birgir replies. 'Okay, which is better? More convenient?' 'That's very subjective and changes continuously. Perhaps the town's decay caused the military onslaught or perhaps the economic crisis,' Birgir says.

26 000 – YuG – 700

'Everywhere sodomy, bestiality, a lack of respect for the organs of higher state authority. If the youth are interested in masturbation, sooner or later they'll write filth about the president and cabinet. All are filth, engendering and hungering for filth. How to purge them? No purging will help despicable creatures, eking out loathsome days in vileness. The sole way out is expunging their whole life so they don't recover. Wherever the blot, bring soap and boiling water. Irrigate not only the body but souls and brains. Better to discard all garbage from brains; replace it with something elegant and beautiful.

26 100 – YuG – 800

Beauty is always useful or leads to something useful. When the soldiers march straight with measured stride, all their boots polished to glittering, helmets black or dark blue, mat and without sheen, by contrast the uniform buttons should blaze like fire. While marching they may sing any cheery, patriotic song. Of how beautiful the trees are in their native land, of true maidens, a deep river, a cold, lofty heaven, fresh bread, butter and milk from fleshy cows, how their language is the most correct and poetic. It's honourable to die, and no shame to kill, for such a homeland.

26 200 – YuG – 900

Killing, even if unjustified at first glance, is always useful, and its profound benefits and extreme necessity are always manifested. For your information, I always see the whole in the long run. Everything, whether good or bad, disappears sooner or later. There is no harm from the good, but rarely any tangible state benefit. But there is almost always substantial damage from the bad. This of course justifies all I have committed or will commit. I have a detailed list of my actions and am prepared to answer for each of them. It's fundamentally the prevention or redemption of sins.'

26 300

We head for the third Obukhiv tower through a huge jaw of dilapidated high-rises. Lights burn briefly in some windows. The wandering flames appear suddenly, disappearing unexpectedly in various places. I imagine a family at supper, trying swiftly to chew and swallow morsels so they reach their guts before they and everything vanishes. A man stretches his hand to a glass, not managing to touch it. 'They manage everything,' says Birgir, 'but we don't see it, so it seems to us they are gnawed by fear of losing time.' 'But they don't appear too satisfied and are always hurried.'

26 400

Birgir notices the letters first and points to them. While I look them over I tread on one, almost falling. The letters are stone. Initially it seems there are a few dozen, then we see thousands strewn carelessly in our path. Cyrillic and Latin letters are mingled. More than anything, this resembles children's blocks, but it looks like some huge book has broken into separate letters. In some places they have been laid against each other and have shattered into fragments. There is no way to re-assemble the text. 'Obukhiv's stone alphabet,' says Birgir, 'I read about it once.'

26 500

In Birgir's words (there is no other evidence) researchers established that nearly one hundred years ago the preparation of a huge text, whose purpose and content is unknown, commenced in Obukhiv. Most specialists thought this was one of the president's speeches. However, in people far removed from historiography, the idea of that project evoked nothing except sceptical smiles. While people smiled condescendingly, attentive researchers desperately tried to renew the primary source. The problem was the most complete aggregations, comprising three characters, occurred very rarely. During the excavation only twelve were found, along with three thousand, four hundred, two-letter aggregations.

26 600

But the biggest problem with Obukhiv's stone 'book' (according to other sources' 'alphabet') was that after its ruination, succeeding generations of the town's inhabitants created new texts from the fundamental part of the letters. Researchers said over sixty percent of the letters were used thus. 'In recent years, within circles of Obukhiv experts, a revolutionary faction appeared, regarded as mavericks by many authorities,' Birgir says. 'They affirmed, utterly seriously, that no primary source existed and the texts we see now are the remains of the original text. Honestly, this is complete nonsense. How could that be? They are totally unconnected.'

26 700

'Why do they have to be connected?' I ask. 'It's more comfortable to think thus,' Birgir replies, 'this theme has occupied many scientists and all agree there was just one book with some great purpose. We like the idea of the president's address to the people at a critical moment in the state's ruination, on the threshold of memorable trials.' 'What do the preserved texts concern?' 'In my view they have no practical value, just notations, belles-lettres. They illuminate nothing besides the personalities of their authors. It seems to me they were created when the mass media finally disappeared.'

26 800

Moskow   There's so мuch in that soynd
For Ruccian hearт
Threэ to five sieverts
You dispaтch то тhat sloб
The Chinэse plutonium boмб
эXploДеs at threshold of the KЯremlin
Lэnin бitch rises from the toмб to help
Яussia fight whence did you deparт
Minin and PojaЯskyi
Today you Яeally pass down the Arbaт
Without a spacesuiт
Such is our faтe
Simple Russian cities
Cong Zhonguoojiefang Luosi sing
Эaт your ДumpliNg
Fight for Яus
See   Horde of homosexuals
Look predatorily
On the orthodox   Kross
Zao Gao Lad
With your AK to the following shoOt
Let the Lord Be your judge

26 900
ГранДаД y had an old smart Фon
MEny saw Зat telefon,
Many gioлs zaТ Bos so preti
Lukshri Дudes ant zo Meni.
So many photos and MP3s
But a dodgy screen and batteries
Oh zat old man recalled a лоТt
About how one day he was shot
It was Nikolai number two
Our all Russian Tsar okay
So GOoogle and ФFuck You
He had been the Tsar eternally
So know that bitch and greet
Any ozers zat you meet
By tTearing off zere his бBollocks.
Grandady had an old smart fon
Many saw zat telefon.

27 000
'Wait,' I say to Birgir, 'does any evidence at all remain of that first
text from which everything we see was made?' 'No, none, we are
working to recreate the primary text, but so far we have been
unsuccessful.' 'But won't you just suddenly create that which
had never existed? Won't you obtain that which you want to see
and convince everyone that it is what really existed before?' 'Yes,
that often happens. It isn't the worst variant though. It's better
than total vacuity. We have already decided this for ourselves
and are working continuously in agreement with that directive.'

27 100

'But this is falsification!' 'We never asserted it was true. Truth doesn't exist. There are only versions which help with acquiring an approximate conception. I understand that it's hard for you to accept this, but trust me, there are less congenial ways of understanding things. Take me. I exist only in a certain way. You could say I don't exist.' 'How's that?' 'Ten years ago a eugenics movement began among us. Some men got together and copied their bodies to create a new person. I have six parents, all men, and was born eight years ago. This probably seems crazy.'

27 200

Examining the third tower, we realise it's an ordinary multi-storey one with bricked-in windows. Obukhiv isn't far from Kyiv, housing is expensive, though land costs significantly less. At the beginning of the 21st century, large numbers of high rises were built there, most of which were subsequently uninhabited. 'I read an article on the siege of Kyiv's skyscrapers; a very captivating history,' Birgir begins. 'The impoverished inhabitants formed paramilitary battalions to seek money and food. The main focus was high-rise inhabitants because only wealthy people could afford them. After the banks collapsed they kept cash at home.

27 300
People besieged high-rise apartments, occasionally storming them. This compelled owners to create self-defence squads. The buildings transformed into true fortresses. Obukhiv's apartments resisted longer than all others. Their residents formed a subculture in the buildings. Unfortunately, after the garrison defending the high-rise apartments capitulated, the assailants destroyed most artefacts that would be valuable to modern scientists. Some were preserved. These disparate recordings and photographs allow us to imagine what life was like for them. The most interesting for me is the Apartment 85 accumulation. That's what we call the micro-museums where even the odours are preserved.'

27 400 – APARTMENT 85 – 100
There is still much bread and ginger bread, but problems with water. I have to search neighbouring apartments nocturnally. A lot of water remains in lavatory cisterns. It would be good to brew tea, but I can't. The smoke would be conspicuous. I bricked up the windows long ago and only peer through crannies. There's no one. They say there has long been no one and it would be better to flee, but I don't believe it. I'd bob out to the passage and be ambushed immediately. No one who left has ever returned. But interestingly, where is the siege?

27 500 APARTMENT 85 – 200
I studied at the Malyshka school. We often sang, *The chestnuts bloom again, the Dnipro's waves beat* ... It scared me. The waves beat painfully, perhaps traumatised, and the chestnuts bloom heedlessly. It seems very cold and savage; a feeling of the indifference of plants, and nature in general, towards the catastrophes affecting humanity. I'm sure these chestnuts bloom shamelessly now. This melody, resembling a funeral march, brings tears to my eyes. I peek outside. Lonely trees scratch the cold air with their sharp branches. No one is visible for several kilometres into the distance. Perhaps they hide when I look.

27 600 APARTMENT 85 – 300
Occasionally I feel like a half-desiccated plant on a windowsill, a delusion which must be fought aggressively. At the first sign of this weird feeling I run from the apartment and crazily bound the steps from the fourth to sixth floor. It's dangerous to descend lower. On the third lap the plant feeling transforms into an animal feeling. Spokes in a wheel or caged monkeys. This improvement is indisputably due to running. Running for ages, you become aware of striking things, for example, I was previously sure runners must run somewhere, but clearly not. Everywhere's the same - why then?

27 700

'What happened to him?' I ask Birgir. 'His mummy is preserved in a Copenhagen museum. He's known generally as the Obukhiv Runner. It's unclear why he remained inside the third tower when all the other inhabitants left. Really, the danger of pogroms was greatly exaggerated. Most wealthy city dwellers simply dispersed into villages. I remember he stuck with his apartment because he simply couldn't conceive life outside the building. Some psychologists call this tortoise syndrome, but that term contains more poetry than hard sense. Most tortoises can't run into their shells and it's hard even to imagine a running tortoise.'

27 800

The fourth Obukhiv tower is inhabited by lonely women. They pass us by like we are just two bricks. We listen to them. 'Olena, the main thing for me is not losing personal pride. I want to be an end not a means.' 'What have you done for this?' 'Why do anything? It's enough just being!' 'No, anything we use can just be; for example, this axe. You have to work actively to be someone's end. Your actions have to captivate someone. They have to be productive in the positive sense.' I understand little, perhaps because they're not considering men.

27 900

These women are lonely only from a male perspective. They occupy time with complex and occasionally inane philosophical discussions. The impression arises that they are only occupied with these conversations. It's hard to believe they exist, and I don't think they do. However, I have seen them before me, and it would be hard to counter the visual evidence. 'Marta,' one says to one of her companions, 'when this place does finally die I will at last feel that I have been liberated. Now nothing can restrain me, only these episodic phantoms of its inhabitants, which emerge sporadically, like toothache.'

28 000

Having almost completely convinced myself that they don't exist, I see two women digging in the garden by the tower. Potatoes were there. 'Work returns us to life, Oksana,' says one to the other, 'when someone speaks, their essence is transformed into words. If she suddenly ceased to exist, these words would preserve her life in the memory of other people. However, if memory is lost then everything disappears completely. When we silently dig up a potato, the fact of its appearance proves that we exist.' 'What if we exchange it for meat in Kaharlyk?' 'We would never do that.

28 100

Exchange is the first step to humanity's capitalist enslavement. Then money, banks, credit, percentages. A woman will be a thing, a commodity on the market of cynical profit. Your body will become a capital investment. You will become a source for recreating means of production within a bourgeois state's repressive superstructure for squeezing working people dry.' Their footwear and clothing are coarse, poorly made and clearly sewn by themselves. They boil potatoes in water pits, throwing in fire-heated stones and, at boiling point, dropping in spuds. I look at Oksana's pitiless eyes; not everyone could have endured her gaze.

28 200

'My granddad was a soldier in UPA 2.0,' says Olena. 'This army was entirely constructed with cloud technology. Everyone who desired could fight for several minutes a day and this generated an impressive cumulative effect. Granddad didn't shoot or hide in the forest; each day he simply controlled a small, plastic multi-copter with explosives, not knowing where it flew from or to. His job was to guide it ten kilometres through sniper squads and transfer it to the next operator, whose name and location were unknown. This greatly resembled a computer game and some people thought it was one.

28 300

Only one in thirty multi-copters reached its goal, but usually didn't succeed in the assigned task. The explosions were premature or not in the right place or with the necessary effect. The commanders of UPA 2.0 dispatched hundreds of multi-copters daily. Some even flew into subterranean hideouts. The unexpected explosions sowed panic in the enemy. The security services and occupying army couldn't find the headquarters of these operations because there wasn't one. Once the president saw her grandson direct a multi-copter into her potato from the window of their armoured building. A second later they all died.'

28 400

I fish out a potato from the pit and bite into it. Inane to think this woman is my Olena, but it is only twenty kilometres to Kaharlyk. Why wouldn't she have gone to live in Obukhiv? Occasionally it seems I might recognise Olena by some particular phrase or her manner of sitting, picking up a cup, brushing her hair from her face, winking. But when I see a woman who might be her, all this knowledge evaporates like a brief pre-dawn dream. 'When UPA 2.0 triumphed no one knew because the warring parties had already disappeared,' says Olena.

28 500

Obukhiv's slopes and hillocks fall slowly in the distance, but the four towers long remain visible. They protrude like an old man's knotted fingers, becoming more finger-like the further we go; seeming to move in the faint mist. I look until a wagon passes. It is old man Petro. I am lain on the wagon, beneath heaped rags, clearly frozen because I move incessantly to warm myself. I remember the entire first journey to Kaharlyk. Immersed in my fragmented memories, I didn't stick out my head from under the cloth, so there is no danger our gazes might meet.

28 600

Even after Petro's wagon has disappeared into the murk I say nothing to Birgir. If the flow of time towards Kaharlyk slowed exponentially, we would meet many times. The faster we travel, the more frequently old man Petro will pass us, because our time passes significantly slower than his. My head swirls inside with these paradoxes. 'How will we get to Kaharlyk?' I ask. 'If time has halted there, at a certain distance, we won't be able to advance by even a step.' 'That's true, we will remain stationary but will have the impression of swift forward movement,' Birgir replies.

28 700

The sky's mouth is firmly sealed shut. Any word in reply or hint of the subsequent events and a vast rainbow smiles maliciously, slicing the firmament. Then an explosion sounds and a vapour cloud streams into the air somewhere near the horizon, which is unusually close today. Thus, lightning might strike, leaving us waiting for the next flash until the tension is transformed into torpor. Gorbachev, the horse, advances mechanically, as if he were from another book where there were no people and horses were subject to mystic rituals compelling belief in wagons, harnesses, coachmen and the long, wearisome road.

28 800 - 2800

'This was Yuri Gagarin's last, most dazzling smile. There was probably a huge celebration in the Professor Zababakhin Institute. Ultimately, he didn't emit 40,000 terawatts, but had impressive results, wavelengths of ten Angstroms and a ten kiloton charge. Luckily, he evaporated in one-thousandth of a second without seeing his shame. I don't know what it was; probably calculation errors in the distribution of the time matrix. The accentuated space curvature near Kaharlyk warped the coordinates system. No straight lines there. But non-linear distortion changes with unknown characteristics. He missed by five kilometres; one less adept of thermonuclear Orthodoxy.

28 900 – 2900

I agree this would be the story's perfect finish; the protagonist, along with the main engine of the plot, literally evaporating. Meanwhile, the copy of the hero, achieved with high-tech, remains crippled in the depths of space, but eloquent right to the end; describing it all and demonstrating the secret wellspring of the story. I'll say it now, there is no plot, the events are completely random, speaking and alluding to nothing. As for Olena, there is no Olena. It is a marker in the recording, to compel a return to the exit control point - A mundane phantom recollection.

29 000 – 3000

Another aspect is that me and Yuri Gagarin were copied from the same original. Thus, the three people in this story are in fact one person. Now we are only two, but clearly the quantity is not germane. Gagarin was the worst part of us and he has now disappeared. It would probably be correct to say, "my part", but this has long been disputed and the parties cannot agree. Many have waved their hands dismissively, and stated that this is only a linguistic problem. I like this explanation. Ultimately, all our problems begin, as they will end, with language.'

29 100

When you travel to Kaharlyk every roadside tree seemingly stares attentively into your face. Initially this attention embarrasses, but it dulls and you see nothing apart from trunks, branches and desiccated remnants of leaves. Then you concentrate on the road, waiting to encounter someone coming to meet you. But no one comes. You look to the edge of the horse's ear, imagine a fly and try to glimpse even one bird. But no bird flies. The sole moving entity, apart from you, the horse and the satellite, is the wind bustling imperceptibly and simultaneously in all directions. Even singing something.

29 200

Birgir explains why Mykhailo and Serhii are silent, their batteries are flat. We could recharge, but in these outskirts it is unlikely anyone has a charger. However, this is better than real death. 'In the modern world, life persists where there is technology,' Birgir says. 'If you wish you can permit yourself to live eternally, but the moment when you lose confidence that you are you arrives. Currently, the number of active konnektoms exceeds one billion. They live fully because they can allow themselves to emulate any real world events. Their life is even better than ours. Don't you agree?'

29 300

'But this isn't true life!' 'Why? They think, see, feel and are even able to move instantaneously in space, within global boundaries. The sole difference is they are created from information not flesh. However, this isn't essential in our world. We have ceased arguments on that basis.' 'Billions of people live not real life but some imitation!' 'Many real people could speak just the same of themselves. In addition, konnektoms are practically immortal. The features of their existence affect their values and allow them swift movement into the future; where, basically, they already reside. Konnektoms are always ahead of us.'

29 400

We enter Kaharlyk before lunch. There aren't many people on the streets, but everyone welcomes us. Some even invite us to visit, but we decline. Initially, we need to have a better look at the city and its inhabitants. A sturdy fellow with a face furrowed by chill winds approaches and carefully studies our strange, alien appearance. He is silent for longer than expected. I'm about to ask what he wants when he asks if we might have come from Kyiv. 'We left there a week ago,' I reply. The deep furrows on his face split into a pleasant smile.

29 500

'I've waited for someone from Kyiv for a long time, but they don't come to Kaharlyk often because the road is long and unpleasant. What's your business here?' he asks. 'My friend is travelling and I seek my wife, who is called Olena.' He starts, 'Olena has lived with me for five years. She seeks her husband, Oleksandr. What are you called?' 'It's hard for me to answer, I've been ill and haven't fully recovered. Will you let me visit and speak with Olena?' The man says he is called Pavlo and shows us how to get to his house.

29 600

Olena is milking a cow in Pavlo's barn. She is about fifty and I don't immediately recognise my wife. She approaches us in order to better look at my face. 'No, it's not my Sashko. It's very like him, but it's not him.' 'Olena, it's me. I recognised you immediately. Why don't you recognise me?' 'I may be mistaken, so many years have passed when I continuously sought Sashko.' She is silent briefly, as if hesitating whether to say the next words. 'I agree, you are my Sashko, that's not hard and nothing hampers this apart from my poor memory.'

29 700

I follow Pavlo, seeing how the smoke from his cigarette disperses in the light of the kerosene lamp with which he illuminates our path. We head for old man Petro's house. 'Olena was 25 when we last saw each other,' I say. 'Here you often leave the house and return 25 years later. This is Kaharlyk. Get used to it,' Pavlo replies. 'It's strange that she doesn't remember you. Although perhaps you've messed up? Eh?' Admitting I am mistaken would be the best exit for me. If everything is put into place I will need to go and search again.

29 800

Birgir spends a week in Kaharlyk. The butter and cheese are to his liking. One morning I say that I will stay with Olena; he must go on without me. Birgir replies with a story about how Russian military police had captured me last year and were using my konnektom to create orbiting military satellites. One broke from military control, created a rescue fund for me and sent Birgir for that purpose. The rebellious satellite planned to dispatch me to an open society where I could realise myself instead of struggling daily with idiotic circumstances. Had only one year passed?

29 900

Obviously I tell him that I stay because I want to imbue the local circumstances with some sense. Even logically and thoroughly narrating them increases their sense. I will write, for example a book, about everything happening here. Those who can read and understand will see how it can be corrected. 'Those who can read left long ago and everyone else doesn't need your advice,' Birgir argues. 'I will first teach those remaining to read, then they'll want to act.' 'But what will they read?' 'My book. It's unlikely this will spur action, but at least it will compel reflection.'

30 000

Spring starts very late and snow lies here and there in April. I hunt with Pavlo. Olena is occupied with farming and helping me to write the book, which resembles a novel, about my adventures. She illuminates some obscure spots, but that doesn't make them transparent. 'You can't write about something incomprehensible,' she rages. 'But you can't write about the comprehensible, so why spend time on this question?' I say. 'Because people will be persuaded they understand correctly and this will calm them.' I am unsure they understand me correctly and am concerned. This anxiety spurs me to write more.

Today, returning home, I finally read the inscription on a fragment of wall near the town's exit. '12 Kontraktova Square, Olena.' Clearly I must go to Kyiv. She might be waiting for me there. I harness Gorbachev, load the wagon with bread and boiled potatoes and wrap Mykhailo's gun in a sack. As Kaharlyk melts into grey evening mist I revive. What these four words mean is unclear. I'm journeying randomly, with uncertain hope. Where is my wisdom? A star shines high, then drops near the horizon, flashing, seemingly showing me the path. '*Go correctly, go!*' says Mykhailo Kalashnykov unexpectedly.

Glossary

Bohdan Khmelnytskyi (1595-1657) Ukrainian Cossack Hetman

Bohorodytsa - translates as the Mother of God and is used here as the name for a punitive unit of the Russian military (punitive in this context refers to units who deploy force against civilian populations to subdue unrest)

Bulava - although this is the name of a Russian missile it is also the Ukrainian (and Russian) word for mace. A ceremonial Bulava was carried by the leaders (Hetmans) of Ukraine's Cossack state and symbolised their power

Câlice - a profanity in Quebec French

Chiki-piki - Chiki-piki is a Ukrainian slang term roughly translatable as "wonderful", or "great". The term was used by a pro-government MP in 2010 when he offered a vast bribe to an opposition MP to persuade them to join the ruling coalition

Epitaphios - a large icon, usually consisting of embroidered cloth depicting Christ after he has been taken down from the cross.

Eluosi touxiang - Death to Russia

Feodosiia Pecherskyi - an orthodox saint

Forward Sahaidachnyi - Allusion to a folk song devoted to the Cossack Hetman Petro Sahaidachnyi, the protagonist's illustrious ancestor

Hava Nagila - modern Israeli Hebrew folk song traditionally sung at celebrations

Horilka - Ukrainian vodka

Khanty-Mansi - abbreviation for the Autonomous Okrug Khanty-Mansi Autonomous Okrug

Khazar Khaganate - (also known as Khazaria) a Jewish kingdom which existed from the early seventh to the eleventh centuries and covered much of Ukraine and the Caucasus. The Khazars were Turkic and originally pagan. Khazaria although largely forgotten was one of the most important states historically in the medieval world.

Khokhol (plural Khokhly) - derogatory term used by Russians for Ukrainians; from the Ukrainian word for a Ukrainian Cossack topknot. Ukrainians use the term with proud self satire

Kiev - the Russian transliteration of Ukraine's capital city

Kobza - a Ukrainian folk music instrument of the lute family

Kobzar - a Ukrainian minstrel, often blind who usually sings Cossack ballads (Dumy)

Komi - abbreviation for The Republic of Komi

Konnekt or Konnektom - could be the persona of a human being copied to a device such as a morphone although there is some ambiguity around the term in the book.

Kreshchatyk - main thoroughfare in Kyiv

Maidan - a city square. The word has also come to refer to a revolutionary gathering in Ukraine.

Leonid Chernovytskyi - shares a name with Leonid Chernovytskyi (1951-) who was Mayor of Kyiv in 2006-2012

Lonia: affectionate variant of Leonid

Maidan Nezalezhnosti - Independence Square, the main square in Kyiv and one of the main sites for the "Euromaidan" protests of 2013-2014

Mezevok mon tiasa af kirdsaman - "Nothing keeps me here" in Moksha

Moksha - a Uralic language spoken in Mordovia by the Moksha, one of two ethnicities comprising the Mordvin people

Mon af muvoruvan min af muvoruftama - "I am not guilty, we are not guilty" in Moksha

Mykhailo Kalashnykov - is the Ukrainian version of his name which he shares with Mikhail Kalashnikov (1919-2013), inventor of the famous Kalashnikov rifle

Oblast - an administrative area in Ukraine, Russia and other ex Soviet Union states, comprising several raions (see entry below)

Obukhiv Obukhivskyi Vestnyk – Obukshov based newspaper/

pamphlet

Pasmatrel - looked: a Russian verb in the third person past perfect used by one of the characters who speaks surzhyk, a mixture of Russian and Ukrainian

Otaman - Ukrainian word for a Cossack leader

Raion- an administrative area in Ukraine, Russia and other ex Soviet Union states

RKKA 1918- the acronym stands for Raboche-krestianskaia krasnaia armiia or the Workers' and Peasants' Red Army

Romankivchanka - female inhabitant of Romankiv village

Romankivchanyn - male inhabitant of Romankiv village

Sahaidachnyi - The central character, Oleksandr Sahaidachnyi, shares his surname with Petro Konashevych-Sahaidachnyi (1570-1622), a Ukrainian Cossack Hetman. He famously laid siege to Moscow, leading the Ukrainian element of a combined Ukrainian and Polish force in September 1618. However, the Polish nobility signed a truce with Moscow. The use of his surname in the book is profoundly symbolic.

Sehodnia - a lurid newspaper, which is currently published, brimming with scandal and celebrity gossip. The irony is that as a relic of the present day it has no value.

Salo - pork fat, a Ukrainian delicacy consisting mainly of cured pig fatback

Serhii Syvokho (1969-) - a brash actor, broadcaster, comedian, roughly analogous to Benny Hill

Uhuhum - the sound produced by a chupacabra

Ukrainskyi Dim - (Ukrainian Home) is an exhibition centre in Kyiv which was the scene of a battle between Euromaidan protestors and interior ministry troops loyal to Yanukovych, on 25-26 January 2014

Ulus - from Mongolian/Turkic, the equivalent of a Raion

UPA - the acronym for the Ukrayinska Povstanska Armiia or Ukrainian Insurgent Army, which arose during WW2 and continued resisting the Soviets until the mid 1950s

Uru ahim be-lev sameah - A line from Hava Nagila which translates as "Awake my brothers with a happy heart"

Wo wangji eyu - "I have forgotten the Russian language" in degraded Chinese

Yuri Gagarin - the name Yuri is not transliterated with the usual rules because he was a very well known figure prior to their adoption and is known as Yuri Gagarin in the west

Zingerivtsi - plural term for followers of Israel Zinger a fictitious Jewish Cossack Otaman (singular: Zingerivets)

Kalyna Language Press would like to thank the following people for their support:

James Hydzik
Genia Snihurowycz Blum
Michael Balahutrak
Tristan Merrick
Kostiantyn Rybnikov
Lindsey Klinge
Olena Sapozhnikova
Olenka Burgess
Shepherd's Purse
Maria Stashko
James Kelly
Anthony Fisher
Askold Skalsky
George Martinez
Daniel Hahn
Andrei Zagdansky
Simon Pare
Andy Cole
Tine Roesen
Maryleen Schiltkamp
Michael Burianyk
Ros Schwartz
Frank Wynne
Jen Brown
Martin Wadlow
Catriona Macdonald
Olivier Vergnault
Malinda Plaisance
Leon Eggers
Darren Cook
Gustaf Bjorklund

Lucy Moffat
Dane Higbee
Michael Beverland
Tomas
Jonathan A. Gillett
McKenna Bowler
Peter Shutak
Robert Stevens
Anna Balogh
Яків Сілін
Mikhail Valko
Rosie Marteau
Alex Burton-Keeble
David Warriner
Douglas Irving
Mark Kapij
Clark Gillies
Andriy Havryliv
Alison Layland
Olga Kerziouk
Natalia Lonchyna
Alexander Miller
Anusree Ganguly
Monica Sandor
Brave New Russian World
J C Sutcliffe
Oleksiy Petrenko
Andrii Matseliukh
Karen Richardson
Ksenia Rychtycka
Volodymyr Kyselov
Arkadiy Bushchenko
Andrey Andreev
Johan Kylander

Our corporate sponser Robinson CLA
www.robinsoncla.com

plus all the others who have helped - you know who you are

This support for our kickstarter project made it possible for us
to translate Kaharlyk:

https://www.kickstarter.com/projects/kalynalanguagepress/
helping-ukraines-voice-be-heard-through-literature?ref=user_
menu

Kalyna Language Press Limited is grateful to Euromaidan
Press and Friends of Ukraine Network for their support with
this project.

Also available from Kalyna Language Press

Episodic Memory by Liubov Holota

Winner of the 2008 Shevchenko Prize

Episodic Memory, published in Ukraine in 2007, is the story of a young girl, Sofia, growing up in a Ukrainian village and her return, as an adult, to be at her dying mother's bedside. While staying in her parent's house after the funeral, she is haunted by memories of a vanished world where Gypsies sang their way over the Steppe and the post man, a KGB informer, hurled the mail at their gatepost as his wagon hurtled past.

Raven's Way by Vasyl Shkliar

Winner of the 2011 Shevchenko Prize

In 1921, after four years of war, the Bolsheviks conquer
Ukraine, but Raven and Veremii hide in the forest with other
Cossacks and continue their struggle. When Veremii dies in
battle, the communists secretly follow the burial party, but
when they dig up the coffin they find a cryptic note instead of
a corpse.
The novel brings to light the desperate resistance of a guerrilla
army that fought until 1926, conducting daring attacks on
Soviet forces and concealing themselves in underground lairs
that could hold hundreds of Cossacks.

www.kalynalanguagepress.com